Readers love
Speed Dating the Boss
by SUE BROWN

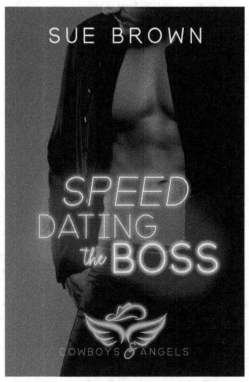

"I was completely caught up in the story from the first page to the last. It was compelling and just about perfect."
—Joyfully Jay

"Sue Brown did an amazing job on this book and I look forward to more by Sue in the future."
—Gay Book Reviews

"I loved this story and was so glad to see Dan find the love he has been looking for."
—Scattered Thoughts and Rogue Words

By SUE BROWN

Chance to Be King
Falling for Ramos
Final Admission
The Layered Mask
The Next Call
The Night Porter • Light of Day
Nothing Ever Happens
The Sky Is Dead
Stitch
Stolen Dreams
Waiting

COWBOYS AND ANGELS
Speed Dating the Boss
Secretly Dating the Lionman

DREAMSPUN DESIRES
#44 – The Fireman's Pole

FRANKIE'S SERIES
Frankie & Al
Ed & Marchant
Anthony & Leo
Jordan & Rhys
Frankie & Friends Anthology

THE ISLE SERIES
The Isle of… Where?
Isle of Wishes
Isle of Waves

ISLAND MEDICS
Island Doctor
Island Counselor

MORNING REPORT
Morning Report
Complete Faith
Papa's Boy
Luke's Present
Letters From a Cowboy
Letters From a Cowboy
Anthology

Published by DREAMSPINNER PRESS
www.dreamspinnerpress.com

SUE BROWN

SECRETLY DATING the LIONMAN

REAMSPINNER PRESS

Published by

DREAMSPINNER PRESS

5032 Capital Circle SW, Suite 2, PMB# 279, Tallahassee, FL 32305-7886 USA
www.dreamspinnerpress.com

This is a work of fiction. Names, characters, places, and incidents either are the product of author imagination or are used fictitiously, and any resemblance to actual persons, living or dead, business establishments, events, or locales is entirely coincidental.

Secretly Dating the Lionman
© 2018 Sue Brown.

Cover Art
© 2018 Kanaxa.
Cover content is for illustrative purposes only and any person depicted on the cover is a model.

Trade Paperback ISBN: 978-1-64080-652-8
Digital ISBN: 978-1-64080-651-1
Library of Congress Control Number: 2018906773
Trade Paperback published November 2018
v. 1.0

Printed in the United States of America

This paper meets the requirements of
ANSI/NISO Z39.48-1992 (Permanence of Paper).

To Tyler, my beautiful white Staffy, who died as this story was being written. We all miss you, Stinky-bum!

A huge thank you to Robyn who read my first draft late one night over large mugs of latte and Vegemite and toast.

CHAPTER 1

CRIS PETERS fumbled to make the call, not willing to take off his gloves in the icy chill of the evening, but the touch screen defeated him, and he had to remove one glove. The second he pressed Send, Cris tucked the phone under his ear and pulled his glove back on. He waited impatiently for the call to connect.

"Hello?" A deep male voice rumbled in his ear and reminded Cris why he'd been attracted to Paul in the first place.

"Hi, Paul. It's Cris Peters."

"Oh yeah. Hi."

Cris couldn't fail to notice the mixture of wariness and indifference in Paul's voice. He'd already canceled one date with Paul, and he was not going to appreciate Cris doing it again simply because his idiot manager couldn't sort out his schedules. He sighed and launched into an explanation of why he had to rearrange their first date again.

Five minutes later Cris no longer had a date to rearrange. Paul had better things to do with his Saturday night than wait in for a guy who wasn't interested, and no amount of apologies would convince him otherwise.

"You're a stripper, not a surgeon. It's not life or death if you don't turn up for work," Paul sneered as he disconnected.

"It's the difference between a bed and the streets, asshole," Cris snapped, but Paul had already gone, and he was left talking to himself.

Cris sighed as he slipped his phone back into his pocket. He really needed a beer, so he pushed open the door to Cowboys and Angels and was immediately hit by a wave of noise and heat and the seventies rock music that blasted out to deafen anyone within a five-block radius. The bar was packed with men ready to drink away their Friday night. A year ago he'd never have thought he'd be seeking a night out at Cowboys and Angels, a blue-collar bar a few blocks from where he lived. It had an extensive list of great beers, but with a reputation for barroom brawls, it wasn't a place where Cris had wanted to spend his nights off. He shook his ass to screaming women for a living. He preferred a quiet evening out with his buddies.

But times had changed, and he came in without more than a quick look around to see if any fights were brewing. There were still skirmishes, but Dan, the new owner, stopped them before more than a few fists flew. The former cause of most of the trouble worked behind the bar now. Between her studies and her work, Ariel, the owner's daughter, no longer had time to stir up the clientele.

He pushed through the crowd toward the bar and greeted some of the customers as he passed.

"Lionman!" One of the men clapped him on the back, and he staggered. Fortunately Cris had excellent reflexes, and he recovered his footing and pasted a smile on his face for the young construction worker who'd accosted him.

"Pat. Good to see you, man."

"My girl saw your show last week." Pat laughed raucously, and his friends joined in. "Now she wants me to dress up in a jockstrap, a cowboy hat, and a ginger wig."

Cris remembered that show, and he remembered Pat's woman, all lush curves and huge dark eyes. "You're a lucky man, Pat." He winked at him. "If you want me to give you lessons on how to strip…."

Pat's friends whistled and jeered, and Pat flushed but grinned good-naturedly. "Maybe I will." He managed a bad hip shimmy.

Cris grinned and left behind a still wildly blushing Pat and a chorus of whistles and cheers. He pushed his way through to the bar and waved at Dan, who came over with a smile and a raised eyebrow.

"Aren't you supposed to be working tonight?" he asked as he pushed a beer across the bar.

Cris took a long swallow. "Mix-up with the schedule. They want me tomorrow night instead."

"Didn't that happen last weekend?"

"And the one before that." Cris rubbed his eyes tiredly. He hadn't been thrilled to discover yet again that the manager of his strip club, Forbidden Nightz, had screwed up his weekend with little more than an apologetic smile and an indifference to how it might affect his life. "Marlon's fuckin' useless, man. And my date didn't appreciate being canceled twice."

"You ought to come and work for me." Dan winked at him.

Cris took another swallow of the honey-based beer. "I keep telling you, you don't pay enough." He grinned to mitigate the sting.

Dan had been suggesting almost since they met that Cris come work at Cowboys and Angels, but Cris's answer was always the same. He could make way more money in tips stripping than he could behind the bar, and he needed every cent just to pay his rent at home and at the studio to indulge in his first love—his painting. Cris stripped to live, and as the red-maned Lionman he was very successful, but the manager's disorganization was messing with his head.

Dan just snorted and handed him a beer. Then he went away to serve another customer. If Dan was on duty, Cris never paid for a drink at Cowboys and Angels. He protested, but Dan ignored him. Cris had helped a friend of Dan's at the strip club when she became unwell. As far as Dan was concerned, Cris was golden. Appropriate, really. Cris had a flaming mane of unruly red hair, hence Lionman as his stage name. But tonight Cris felt more like a stray alley cat than the king of the jungle.

Cris finished his first drink, picked up the second, and turned around to look at the room. He recognized a lot of the customers now, and a couple of them gave him a sloppy wave. There was a scuffle as the wave smacked into another guy's face, but they settled down after a bellow from Dan. Cris turned away hastily. He didn't want to attract the attention of one of the men. He'd met him before, at a speed-dating evening held at Cowboys and Angels, and he had one foot and the rest of his body in the closet. Mr. Seventeen. Why the guy attended the event, Cris had no idea. Mr. Seventeen, whose name was Mikey, panicked every time he saw Cris. As though Cris would out anyone against their will. He knew more secrets than a hairstylist.

The door opened, letting in a blast of cold air. Cris saw Mikey—no, not Mikey, but someone who looked like him—come in and look around. He took off his hat and swept a hand through his thick hair, leaving it rumpled. He was older than Mikey, and he wore a deep frown. For some reason Cris itched to smooth the rumpled hair and the frown. The patrons started to grumble, so the man hastily shut the door and headed over to Mikey, who didn't look pleased to see him. Cris watched curiously as they had what looked like a heated discussion. The older guy pointed to the door, but Mikey shook his head and took a step back, his expression resolute.

"Another beer?" Dan asked.

Cris dragged his gaze away from the tableau. "Thanks. Who's Mikey talking to?"

Dan flicked a glance their way. "Bennett. Mikey's older brother. He's probably trying to get Mikey home before he gets himself into trouble."

"Does it work?"

"Mikey gets into trouble just by breathing."

"They look like each other," Cris observed.

"Yeah, but in personality, they're oil and water. Bennett is a steady guy. He works for the family business."

Cris looked at Bennett. His face was set and angry as he tried to persuade Mikey to leave. "And Mikey's the prodigal son?"

"Something like that."

From the angry set of his shoulders as he stormed toward the door, Bennett had given up on his wayward brother.

"Lionman!"

Cris rolled his eyes, pasted a smile on his face, and turned to face Gideon, the former owner of Cowboys and Angels, who strode across the room to him. Cris was just over six feet tall and muscled, but Gideon could make three of him. He made Cris feel small, which was a rare feeling, and Cris wasn't sure he liked it. "Hi, Gideon."

He was always wary around Gideon. He'd made the mistake of showing his interest in Dan just as Gideon declared his own. Dan was head-over-heels in love with Gideon, and there had never been any real contest, but Gideon obviously viewed Cris as a rival.

Gideon smiled at him. "Aren't you working tonight?"

"Another mix-up with the schedules," he said flatly.

Gideon frowned. "This not the first time, is it?"

"No." Cris leaned against the bar. "Getting tired of it, you know? Now they want me to work tomorrow night, and I'd planned to go out. But I've gotta work. I can't afford to turn down a shift."

"You should come and work for me."

"Thanks, man." Cris meant it. "I'm grateful for the offer. It's just the money. I can earn a lot more at the club, and I need it to pay my rent. No offense," he added hastily.

"None taken."

Gideon eyed him speculatively, but Gideon just said, "Enjoy your evening. Gotta be visible or Dan gets annoyed."

Cris hid his amusement until Gideon turned away. When Dan became the manager, he'd insisted Gideon show his face in the bar. Gideon complained loudly to anyone who would listen, but they all knew he'd do anything for Dan. Now Dan was the owner, it seemed he still had Gideon on a tight leash.

Cris turned and waved his glass at Dan. "'Nother?"

"Is that a question or a request?"

"Just fill it up."

Dan took the glass and refilled it with Cris's favorite beer. "Do I need to get Gideon to pour you home?"

"I'm not wasted on three beers, dude," Cris protested.

"'Kay. He can give you a ride home if you need it."

Cris mumbled his thanks, and Dan went off to serve someone else. Cris sighed. He was used to being the focus of attention on stage, not the sad sack at the bar. Maybe it was time he went home and crashed out in front of the Hallmark Channel to watch sappy romances.

"I really am that sad," he muttered into his glass.

"Lionman!"

Cris cursed under his breath. Thanks to Gideon's incessant use of his stage name, no one called him Cris. He turned to see Mikey lurching toward him and hastily put down his glass. "Lionman." Mikey wafted beer fumes in Cris's face as he swayed.

Cris caught him by the biceps, afraid of getting smacked in the head. "Whoa, big man, steady."

Mikey didn't seem to notice. "You look sad, Lionman. Are ya sad?"

He gave Cris a sloppy smile and tried to pat his face, but only succeeded in smacking Cris in the nose. Christ, it was early for the guy to be that trashed. No wonder his brother was trying to get him home.

Cris caught Mikey's wandering hand before he could inflict more damage. "I'm okay, Mikey. Just fed up."

"You don' wanna be tha'. You gotta be happy, like me."

There were a lot of ways Cris could have responded, considering Mikey was the unhappiest man he'd ever met, but Mikey meant well, and Cris made an effort to smile. "Thanks, Mikey. I'm gonna take a leak and go home now. You take care."

Mikey took a moment to focus on him as his eyes seemed to want to go in different directions. Then he blinked, focused, and nodded. "Okay. 'Night."

Cris squeezed Mikey's arm, ensured he was steady on his feet, and headed off to the bathroom. He pushed the door and was about to walk in when he was shoved from behind, and for the second time that evening, he struggled to stay on his feet.

CHAPTER 2

THANKS TO reflexes honed by years of dancing, Cris managed to avoid falling flat on his face. He stumbled and spun on his heel, ready to lay out his attacker, only to have to fend off Mikey as he clumsily tried to stick his tongue down Cris's throat. Cris turned his face away and struggled to get free, but Mikey's hands were all over him, groping and holding him in place.

"For heaven's sake, Mikey, stop." Cris managed to tear his face away to shout at Mikey, who looked wounded.

"You don't want to kiss me?" Mikey sounded confused.

Cris propped him against the wall to keep him upright but also to keep him at arm's length. "One, this is Cowboys and Angels, not a gay bar, and I'm not getting beat up because you're drunk. Two, I like to be asked. Three, you're drunk, and I'm not taking advantage of any guy who's trashed. Four... oh hell, get to the stall now."

He propelled Mikey there in the nick of time and recoiled as Mikey retched and gagged. It was a great way to spend his Friday evening—holding back a dude's hair as his liquor made its inevitable reappearance.

There was a fifth point, but Mikey didn't need to hear it at the moment. Mikey was too young for Cris—too young and too closeted. Cris preferred guys with mileage under the hood. That's why he'd liked Dan. But now Dan and Gideon were married and sickeningly in love. Cris thought of Mikey's brother. Now *he* had mileage under his hood, but Cris had left lusting after straight guys behind in his teenage years.

The door opened behind him, but he remained focused on the miserable man hunched over the john.

"Do you need help?" Gideon asked.

Cris looked over his shoulder. "He could do with some water when he's done puking."

"I'll bring a bottle."

Gideon vanished as Mikey groaned and heaved again, and Cris
rubbed his back and held his hair out of the way until he was done. It
wasn't the first time he'd done that, and it probably wouldn't be the
last. Finally Mikey raised his head and wiped his streaming eyes.

"Done?" Cris asked.

"Think so." Mikey avoided looking at Cris and lurched out
of the stall as Gideon came in with an uncapped bottle of water. He
accepted it, took a mouthful, swished it around, and spat into the sink.

Gideon leaned against the wall and waited for Mikey to finish.
"Time you went home, son. I'll give you a ride."

"I'm…." Mikey trailed off under Gideon's hard glare.

"You're done," Gideon said flatly.

"I'm done too," Cris said. "I'll ride with you."

"You don' need to babysit me," Mikey grumbled as Cris
manhandled him out of the bathroom.

Cris ignored him. He just wanted to pour Mikey into his bed and
go seek his own. Dan gave him a thumbs-up and mouthed, "Thanks,"
as they walked by.

Mikey's buddies looked wary as they saw him in Cris's company,
but when they came over and caught the smell of vomit, they backed
away with a hurried, "See you tomorrow."

Cris snorted and steered him out of the bar. The icy wind seared
down Cris's lungs, but Mikey didn't seem to notice. He was asleep as
soon as he slumped into Gideon's Nissan, and Cris fought to put the
seat belt around him.

"At least he's not puking," Gideon commented as he sat in the
driver's seat, but Cris noticed he didn't offer to help.

Cris sat beside Mikey just in case the situation changed, but
Mikey stayed asleep all the way to his apartment. Mikey lived close to
Cris, so when Gideon deposited them in front of Mikey's apartment,
Cris said he'd take it from there.

Gideon looked over his shoulder with a worried look on his
face. "Are you sure? He's not a small guy. I'll help you get him to
his door."

"Okay. Help me get him out of the car." Cris shook Mikey.
"Come on, dude. Time to move."

Mikey grumbled something incoherent and snuggled against Cris's shoulder.

Cris rolled his eyes. "You're not sleeping here."

Gideon leaned in and hauled Mikey out without ceremony. "Come on."

"Does he live alone? We'll need his keys."

Cris held him upright while Gideon patted Mikey down until he found his keys in his pocket. Mikey tried to slap Gideon's hand away, but Gideon told him to pipe down, and thankfully Mikey subsided with a huff against Cris.

"Dude, don't breathe on me." Cris turned his head away from the rank waft.

Between them they maneuvered Mikey into the apartment building and into the elevator. It creaked and whined up to the seventh floor, and Cris let out a relieved breath when the doors opened.

"I think I'll walk down," Gideon said as they looked for apartment 702.

"Me too," Cris said fervently.

Gideon fumbled with the keys until he found the right one. Then he opened the door and looked at Cris. "Are you sure you don't want me to wait?"

"I'm sure. I'll be five minutes behind you. I'll find his bed and a trash can, and after that he's on his own."

"Okay then."

Gideon headed back the way they'd come, and Cris took a firmer grip on Mikey.

"Okay, Mikey. Bed for you."

Mikey's head lolled, but Cris heard his "I ain't easy."

Cris snorted. "Neither am I, dude."

He got him inside, retrieved the keys, and closed the front door.

"Mikey, where the hell have you been? And who the hell are you?"

Cris peered around Mikey's head to find the older version of Mikey glaring at him. Bennett was not quite as tall as Mikey but broader across the shoulders, and his thick dark-brown hair was shot with the occasional gray strand.

There's mileage under his hood. The guy was everything Mikey wasn't—mature and sexy, even with the frown.

Mikey raised his head. "Hey, Benny. Wha' you doin' here?"

Bennett stepped closer and wrinkled his nose. "Are you drunk? I told you to come home."

A woman suddenly appeared. She was very young, with long dark-blonde hair tumbling about her face. "We've been so worried, Mikey."

Cris couldn't help noticing the tension that flooded through Mikey, so he turned Mikey away from them. "Who are these people?"

Mikey refused to look at him. "Benny's my brother. And Julianne is...."

Julianne joined them by the door. "I'm Mikey's girlfriend. Pleased to meet you."

She held out her hand. Not convinced Mikey's legs would hold him, Cris changed his grip on Mikey to the other hand and shook hers. "Cris Peters."

Benny didn't offer his hand, and as the silence grew awkward, Cris decided he'd played Good Samaritan long enough. "I've gotta be going. You're in good hands, Mikey." He let go, and Mikey swayed. Benny grabbed him with a disgusted grunt, which Cris ignored, along with a whimpering plea from Mikey. "G'nite."

Cris held out the keys to Julianne and left Mikey to his fate. Then he closed the front door behind him with a sigh of relief and strode away as fast as he could.

"Wait! Peters!" Bennett's booming voice echoed around the hallway.

Cris closed his eyes. He'd been so close. As Bennett jogged to him, he stopped and turned. "Yes, Benny?"

"It's Bennett. Only my family call me Benny. I don't know you. Why did you come home with my brother?" He loomed in Cris's space, but Cris refused to take a step backward.

"He was drunk and sick. I live near here, so I brought him home."

"Is that all?" Bennett demanded.

Cris raised an eyebrow. "What do you mean?" He knew damn well what Benny was asking, but he was damned if he was going to answer.

Bennett crossed his arms and scowled at Cris. He'd be a good-looking man without the frown. Cris wondered how old he was. "Where was he?"

"Cowboys and Angels. You know he was there. I saw you earlier."

"He stayed there?"

"Yeah," Cris said shortly. He couldn't mistake the look of relief in Bennett's expression. No wonder Mikey was so mixed up. He had a girlfriend, and his brother was a homophobe. "I've got to go."

"Well, thanks for taking care of him." From his sour tone, Bennett obviously needed to work on his people skills.

"No problem," Cris said shortly. He left Bennett where he was, feeling like the man was boring two holes in the back of his head.

He wasn't surprised to find Gideon's car still outside the apartment. He opened the door and looked in. "Taxi?"

Gideon nodded. "I had a feeling… I thought you might be glad for a ride."

Cris got into the passenger seat and sighed with relief. "Appreciate it."

"Mikey can be a handful when he's liquored up."

From the drama Cris had just left behind, *handful* was an understatement. "Did you know he has a girlfriend?"

There was a long pause, and then Gideon answered. "Yeah, I know."

"Do you know his brother?" Cris asked curiously.

"Bennett? I know him. He doesn't come in Cowboys and Angels much. Mikey's one of the guys. Bennett's management, if you get my meaning."

"He wasn't happy to see me with his brother."

Gideon snorted. "I'll bet. He's got a stick up his ass."

"Between him and the girlfriend, no wonder Mikey's confused."

"Maybe."

Cris turned to look at Gideon, his curiosity piqued by the cryptic answer. "Maybe?"

"I've known the Petrovskis a long time. Bennett's an asshole, but he adores his little brother. He's always there for him, and he's the one I usually call if Mikey needs a ride home."

"Do you think he knows Mikey is gay?"

"I'm almost sure he does. Mikey's not doing a good job of hiding it."

It was Cris's turn to snort. "That's an understatement, especially if he throws himself at the nearest guy every time he's drunk."

"But he didn't, did he?"

"Didn't what?"

"Throw himself at the nearest guy. He threw himself at a gay guy."

"You mean I'm safe?"

"He trusts you."

"He doesn't know me, Gideon. We've spoken half a dozen times, if that. I can't be responsible for his safety."

Gideon sighed as they pulled up outside Cris's apartment. "I know, Lionman. I'll talk to him next time he's in. Thanks for taking care of him this evening."

"No problem. Thanks for the ride." Cris opened the door, but before he got out, he turned to Gideon. "Mikey's a good guy, but he's not my type."

"I know. Dan's more your kind of guy."

There was no point avoiding the issue. If Gideon hadn't been on the scene, he would have made a play for Dan. "Yeah, but he's stupid in love with you."

Gideon didn't even try to hide his smug expression. "Yeah, he's all mine."

Cris shook his head. "I don't know what he sees in you."

He shut the car door on Gideon's outraged snort. Gideon was tall, handsome, wealthy, and had a heart of gold—pick of the damn litter. He wasn't Cris's type either.

As Cris jogged across the sidewalk toward the door, another face popped into his head—someone angry, brooding and sexy as hell. He would have licked Bennett Petrovski all over. *Well done, Cris. You've fallen for the homophobe.*

CHAPTER 3

"THEY'RE LIVELY tonight," Raymond warned.

He'd just finished his set and was naked apart from his jockstrap and a healthy number of bills tucked into the screaming pink satin. Raymond grabbed a towel and wiped the sweat from his face and the back of his neck.

Cris flipped his feet into his boots. For his next set he was pretending to be an explorer. He wore the hat, jacket, and pants, all of them easy to rip off. "Anyone I should watch out for?"

"All of them. They're good with the tips, but handsy too."

"Thanks for the warning."

Cris rolled his shoulders, stretched his hamstrings, and prepared to give another group of women the performance of a lifetime. He left the dressing room and waited by the stage for his cue. After three years of stripping several times a week, Cris had long since lost his self-consciousness about being naked in front of other people. He still felt the excitement, the anticipation of a new performance, but he had no illusions about what he was. Yes, he danced in his performance, but he wasn't a dancer or an actor. He was a stripper, and a damn good one, and he was honest about what he did for a living. He made good money, and he had fun. When it stopped being fun, he would stop stripping.

There was his cue. As much as he hated "The Lion Sleeps Tonight," it was the perfect opening music for him, and the women roared their approval as he slunk onto the stage. He knew a lot of them by name. Some were there for bachelorette parties, some were there with friends, but all of them loved seeing guys strip down to nothing but their jockstrap. When his friends asked him why he didn't work at gay clubs, Cris told them he went to gay clubs for pleasure, not for work. But the truth was that he could earn more money working here. And he liked that he could work at night and have the rest of the week off to indulge in his painting.

But now the women were cheering their approval, and Cris had to focus his attention on the job at hand. He stalked to the front of the stage, grabbed his hat, and thrust his hands in the air. The cheers were deafening, and Cris smiled broadly. It was going to be a good evening.

By the end of the night, Cris felt he'd been in the ring with a heavyweight boxer. The women were more than handsy, they were full-on mauling, and his body bore the marks to prove it. There was more than one set of scratches down his thighs.

"It's a good thing you don't have a jealous woman at home," Raymond said as Cris dabbed at the scratches with antiseptic. "I have to explain these to Maria every time."

Cris laughed. "It would be harder to explain them to a jealous boyfriend."

"That's true. But it's about time you found yourself another man. How long has it been now?"

Cris winced at a particularly deep scratch. "Too long. What can I do, Raymond? Every time I book a date, Marlon changes my shift. I was supposed to go out tonight, but this is the second time I've canceled on him, and the guy bailed."

Raymond nodded. "He did the same to me. At least my Maria is understanding. It never used to be like this. Andy was a good manager."

Cris pulled on his jeans and sucked in a breath as the denim rubbed his scratches. He should have brought sweats instead. "Dan from Cowboys and Angels wants me to go and work there."

Raymond's eyes opened wide. "The bar near Prospect Park?"

"That's the one. I went there for the speed-dating evening. I've become friends with Dan and his husband." Cris paused as he sucked in another breath to button up his jeans. "It would be regular work, and I know they need the staff, but…."

"The money isn't as good, and you won't have time for your painting?"

"Yeah, although they don't know about the art. This place gives me what I need at the moment… if they could just get their act together and sort out the schedule."

Raymond laughed. "I heard Gideon is rolling in money. You should get him to buy the place and get that pretty girl of his to manage it. She'd keep this place in check."

Cris looked at him curiously. "Have you met Gideon and Ariel?"

"She was at school with my little sister. I met her a couple of times. She's a…."

Cris grinned as Raymond trailed off. "Yes, she is a brat. But now that Dan is the manager, she's working behind the bar. I don't think she gets much time to cause trouble."

"It was about time they took her in hand. She wasn't really friends with my sister. I got the impression she was pretty but spoiled. Larger than life, you know?" Raymond seemed to be choosing his words carefully.

"Just like her father," Cris muttered.

"I never met him."

"He's an older version of his daughter—larger than life and needed Dan to take him in hand. Just like Maria's done with you."

Raymond balled up a sheet of paper and threw it. When it landed squarely in the middle of Cris's chest, Raymond punched his fist into the air. "Score!"

Cris shook his head and pulled on his long-sleeve T-shirt. "You're in the wrong job, my friend. With an aim like that, you should be playing baseball instead of stripping for a living."

Raymond looked a little wistful. "It would have been a dream of mine, but I busted my knee playing football senior year." He pointed to the long scar down his left knee—a white line against his tanned skin.

"Sorry to hear that, man. It must have been hard."

"We all have our dreams." Raymond shrugged eloquently, picked up his backpack, and slung it over his shoulder. "See you next Friday."

"See you then, if the schedule doesn't get changed again."

Raymond saluted and left Cris in the small changing room to pull on his boots. As he finished lacing them, there was a knock at the door, and he called, "Come in." He wasn't used to anyone bothering to knock. Most people just walked in, ignoring the state of undress of the performers. The last person he expected to see was Mikey's brother, Bennett.

"Oh, hi. What can I do for you?" Cris asked a little awkwardly as he got to his feet.

Bennett gave him a curt nod. "Hi. I'm sorry to bother you here, but Mikey didn't know your address and Julianne said you worked here. She's been here before."

Cris nodded and waited for Bennett to carry on. When nothing was forthcoming, he asked, "You wanted to talk to me?"

"I want to talk to you about Mikey."

"I don't really know Mikey," Cris began cautiously. He had the feeling he was about to navigate a minefield without a map. "I only brought him home because he was sick."

"So you haven't spoken to him today?"

Cris shook his head. "I haven't spoken to anyone today. Why?"

Bennett huffed and rubbed his eyes. "He's almost married to Julianne. We're just waiting for them to set a date."

It was on the tip of Cris's tongue to ask if Mikey knew that, but he bit back the words. "That's very nice, but what's it got to do with me?"

"He said something last night that made me think he's been doing things he shouldn't."

Cris ran out of patience. "Why don't you say what you really mean, rather than skirting around the issue? It's been a long day, and I just want to go home and go to sleep."

"Alone?" Bennett snapped.

"Yes, alone, although I don't know what my bed status has to do with you."

"You're not going to be calling my brother to ask if he wants to come over?"

Who the hell had stuck a bug up Bennett's ass? "Let's get something straight before I ram your teeth down your throat. I am *not* involved with your brother. I've never been involved with Mikey, and I don't intend to start now. I just did him a favor last night bringing him home. Second, if you know your brother is gay, why the hell are you forcing him into an engagement he obviously doesn't want?"

"He's not gay."

"He certainly felt gay when he had his tongue down my throat."

Bennett narrowed his eyes. "I thought you said you weren't involved."

"We're not," Cris pointed out, holding on to his patience by a thin thread. "He was drunk and thought he'd kiss me. I pushed him off and gave him a lecture about consent. Then he threw up. I could hardly leave him there by himself. He was trashed."

"He's drinking too much."

"If he's confused and getting a hard time from home, I'm not surprised he's drinking."

Bennett glowered at him. "He's not getting a hard time. He's been in a relationship with Julianne for five years. They're high school sweethearts, and they're going to get married."

"Does Mikey know that?" Cris gave up trying to be polite.

"He's not gay."

"Who are you trying to convince, me or yourself?" Cris held up his hand against another angry outburst by Bennett. "Look, it's nothing to do with me. If Mikey wants to go through with an engagement to a woman, that's up to him."

"He was fine before you got him all confused."

Cris shook his head. "Do you hear yourself? Is this 2018 or 1957? Have you finished, because I'm done now. I'm tired and want to go home."

"Stay away from Mikey," Bennett snapped.

"Or what?"

Bennett clenched his fist, and Cris held his breath, expecting to get punched. "Or you'll regret it."

"Is that a threat?" Cris mocked.

"It's a promise."

Bennett stalked out of the dressing room, and Cris sat down, more shaken by the encounter than he liked. He hated confrontation, and he wasn't sure whether he believed Bennett would follow through with his threat, but he was obviously angry enough to make the trip to the club. Cris needed to talk to someone, and it obviously wasn't going to be Mikey.

THE NEXT day Cris found himself with an enraptured audience as he told Dan and Ariel about the previous two nights. Gideon had already heard part of the story, but even his eyes widened as Cris relayed Bennett's angry outburst.

Dan whistled. "This explains a lot."

"Hell yes," Ariel agreed. "I thought that boy had the closet door padlocked shut, and now we know why."

"I thought it was his work and the boys here," Dan said.

"It's probably that too. The poor boy's got nowhere he can turn."

"Sticking his tongue down my throat isn't gonna help the situation," Cris said.

Dan nodded. "I'll have a word with him about that. He can't get drunk and approach just any dude. He was lucky it was you."

"That's exactly why he *did* approach Cris," Ariel said. "He knew Cris wouldn't hurt him, and he might get lucky."

Cris snorted. "I like my face as it is. I have no desire to see it rearranged in Cowboys and Angels." There was an odd silence he didn't understand. Dan and Ariel seemed to be doing their best not to look at each other, and Gideon was suddenly intently interested in his coffee. "What did I just say?"

"It doesn't matter," Dan said hastily.

Ariel sighed. "I guess it's all right if you know. I spoke out of turn to a couple of guys here, and they *did* decide to rearrange Dan's face because he was gay. I'll never forgive myself for Dan getting hurt."

Dan wrapped his arm around Ariel's shoulders. "It's okay. It's all over, and you made amends."

Judging from his tight expression, Gideon wasn't so forgiving of his daughter's lapse in judgment, but then he was hellishly possessive of Dan. Cris sought a way to change the subject. "What do I do about Mikey?"

"I don't know," Dan admitted.

"Do you want me to ban him?" Gideon asked.

Cris stared at him. "You'd do that?"

Gideon twisted his lips into a wry smile. "If it keeps the peace."

"But Mikey's been coming here a lot longer than me."

"He's a ticking time bomb," Dan said. "At some point he's going to explode, and I don't want it to be here."

"It's a real shame." Ariel was serious for once. "Mikey's a good man. He'd be so much happier if he could just be true to himself."

Gideon sighed and put down his mug. "I'll talk to him first. We don't want any more trouble here, and I'll warn him of the consequences if he tries anything like that with Cris again."

Cris felt relieved. He'd been worried they wouldn't take him seriously, and he was glad to know they had his back. He wished there were more he could do for Mikey, but he wasn't the one who could help him.

Ariel grinned wickedly at him. "So, tell us about Mikey's brother."

Cris groaned. "He's ready to punch my lights out. I don't know if I'm going to have to look over my shoulder every time I go out. He's got it into his head that I'm Mikey's boyfriend. He told me to stay away or else."

Dan gave him a wry smile. "You won't be in a hurry to be a Good Samaritan again, will you?"

"No, I'll probably dive in again just like I always do." Cris sighed. "This is a new one, though. I normally get thanked by the family, not threatened with bodily harm."

"I'll tell Mikey to warn his brother off." Dan handed Cris a beer.

"It's a bit early to start drinking, isn't it?" Cris asked, although it didn't stop him chugging down a good slug of the cool liquid.

"I think you deserve it, and you're not working tonight."

"I wish I were," Cris admitted. "It would take my mind off the scary brother."

Dan eyed him speculatively. "If you're not busy, and you want something to do, I could use a hand here this evening. Ariel needs a break, and tonight is generally quiet."

Ariel squealed and clapped her hands. "If you say yes, I promise to send every woman I know to stick fifty-dollar bills in your jockstrap."

Cris stared at her. "You know how creepy that sounds, don't you? Especially in front of your father."

"I'm used to it," Gideon said. "I've had a lot of practice."

"I could use the money, but I haven't worked a bar before, so you're gonna need to train me."

"I'll do that," Ariel promised as she rubbed her hands together. "Finish your beer, new minion. It's time to do some real work."

"I do real work," Cris protested.

"Uh-huh."

The snickers from Dan and Gideon did nothing to inspire Cris's confidence. "Is it too late to change my mind?"

Ariel gave a maniacal laugh. "Much too late, minion."

CHAPTER 4

BY CLOSING time, Cris discovered muscles he didn't know existed. He was a fit guy, who worked out every day, but under Ariel's dictatorship, Cris discovered the difference between standing on his feet all day and dancing for a few hours. When the last customers finally left, arms wrapped around each other's shoulders and weaving out the door, Cris gave a sigh of relief and collapsed on the bar.

"How do you feel?" Dan asked as he locked up.

Cris groaned into his folded arms. "I am never gonna be stupid enough to do this again."

"You didn't enjoy it?"

Cris thought about that seriously. "Yeah, I did enjoy it. It's a different kind of interaction with customers, and it's a real pleasure to keep my clothes on for once. But how do you keep going, man? I did not stop working all day."

Dan shrugged. "I've been working the bar since I left high school. It's all I know."

"I thought *my* job was physical."

"It's a different kind of work. I couldn't do what you do."

Cris smirked at him. "Dance or strip?"

"Take your pick. There's no way I'm taking my clothes off in front of hundreds of women."

"That's a real shame. They'd go wild for a bod like yours." Cris swept his gaze over Dan and grinned at the flush that rushed up his neck.

Then he heard a growl behind him. Shit. Of course Gideon had to hear him say that.

Dan rolled his eyes at Gideon. "Down boy. Cris wasn't hitting on me... much."

"He'd better not be," Gideon growled again.

Cris held his hands up. "I wasn't hitting on your boy. I was just pointing out that women would love him. He's got a great body."

"Yeah, he has, and the only one who's going to see how fabulous it is is me."

Gideon shot Dan a heated look that Cris couldn't miss. A look like that was hard on the single man in the room, and Cris shifted uncomfortably.

"What do you need me to do?" All Cris wanted was to go home and crash into bed.

"I'll help Dan close up," Gideon said. "You get on home. You're welcome to come here for regular shifts. You worked harder than a lot of the guys do."

Cris was surprised by Gideon's praise. "I'll think about it. Is it okay if I come by tomorrow and we discuss it?"

"Sure. We'll need to sort out wages for today."

Yawning, Cris rolled his shoulders and stretched. "I'll see you later on."

Dan and Gideon wished him good night, and Cris retreated to the back to collect his coat and order an Uber. When he came back into the bar, the two men were kissing. He waited a moment and then coughed to attract their attention. They broke apart, somewhat reluctantly. Gideon cupped Dan's jaw as though he were the only one in the room.

Cris smiled at them apologetically. "I'm sorry to interrupt, but I need you to let me out of the bar."

Dan blinked a couple of times and then seemed to focus on Cris. "Oh sure, sorry."

Gideon didn't look sorry at all. He looked smug. Cris was pretty sure Gideon was trying to make a point, but he didn't need to. Cris knew exactly who Dan belonged to.

He said good night to both of them and leaned against the wall outside while he waited for his car. He was almost asleep when it arrived.

The driver grinned at him. "Late night?"

"Really long day."

As they drove the short distance to his apartment, Cris thought about the kiss he'd just witnessed. Dan and Gideon were in the honeymoon phase of their relationship, but Cris could see the tenderness between them. He hoped he'd find it himself one day, but it didn't look like it would be soon—and certainly not with someone as young as Mikey. For some reason Bennett crept into his mind, or rather strode in and demanded attention. Bennett was everything that pushed his buttons. Cris sighed and closed his eyes. It was typical that he'd be attracted to a raving homophobe.

CRIS GENERALLY didn't work Mondays. He used them to get his chores out of the way for the rest of the week. He liked the laundromat best, because he used it to catch up on his reading. So he found his favorite machine, loaded his clothes and soap, settled in his favorite seat—yes, he was that predictable—and was deep in his latest thriller when someone said, "Cris?"

He looked up to see Bennett standing in front of him. "Bennett." He really hoped the man wasn't going to cause trouble. The tiny Chinese woman who ran the laundromat wielded a mean broom, and he'd seen more than one troublemaker ejected at the end of it.

"I didn't realize you came here too." Bennett seemed as pleased to see him as Cris was.

Cris spotted Bennett's bag, presumably full of clothes, and was relieved Bennett hadn't been following him. On the other hand, he never remembered seeing Bennett there before. "I come here every Monday, although I'm usually earlier than this. I had a late night working at the bar."

"Cowboys and Angels?"

Cris nodded. "They were shorthanded."

"Was Mikey there last night?" Bennett sounded suspicious, and Cris resisted the urge to tell him to mind his own business.

"No."

"Good. Things aren't right with Julianne, and I told him to sort it out. I'd be pissed if he'd ended up at the bar."

"Why is it any of your business?" Cris didn't hide his unfriendliness.

Bennett scowled at him. "He's my brother."

"Yeah, and he's an adult, so why're you interfering in his relationship?"

"Because he makes bad decisions," Bennett snapped.

Cris squinted up at him and shielded his eyes from the harsh light overhead. "I can understand you looking out for your brother, but surely his relationship is his business, no one else's."

"You don't understand."

"No, I don't," Cris agreed. "I don't know Mikey that well. I've only met him a few times, and we've never talked."

Bennett sat down next to him. "You know each other well enough for him to try and kiss you."

"He was drunk, that's all. He spent most of his time trying to avoid me because he knows I'm gay. There's nothing between us." Cris would say that over and over until Bennett got it into his thick skull.

"I know," Bennett said surprisingly. "We had a long talk yesterday. He's mortified about the kiss."

Cris waved his hand. "Let's forget it. If he remembers anything I said, that's good enough."

"He remembers." Bennett's tone was grim, and Cris had a feeling that if Mikey hadn't remembered, Bennett would have reinforced his lecture.

"As long as he doesn't do it again, we're cool."

"You're not into him?" Bennett asked suspiciously.

Cris sighed. He was really getting sick of this. "No. For the final time I am not into your brother. He's not my type."

"Good. Because he's not gay."

Oh, good God. That was too fucking much. How blind could the man be? Cris took in a deep breath and exhaled slowly. *In. Out.* Bennett's head would make a good punching bag. *In. Out.* He turned to look Bennett in the eyes. "Bennett, I can see you're a decent man, and it's really obvious you love your brother. So why is it so hard to accept that he's gay?"

"He's not—"

"Gay. I know. You keep saying that. But straight men do not stick their tongues down other men's throats. He may be bisexual, he may be pansexual, but he sure ain't straight. No amount of saying it will make it so. And I've got a feeling a lot of those bad decisions you keep talking about were centered around his relationships?"

Cris was totally focused on Bennett. It was easy to see the anger rising as Cris spoke. But it wasn't only anger. It was sadness too. Whatever was going on, it affected Bennett, and Cris didn't know what the hell he could do about it.

"It's none of your business."

"You keep making it my business," Cris pointed out.

Bennett clenched his fists. "Leave my brother alone. Don't come near him again." He stalked out of the laundromat and left Cris staring after him.

It took a few minutes for Cris to realize that Bennett had left his laundry behind. He waited, but Bennett didn't come back for it. Cris looked in the bag at the unwashed clothes and sighed. Then he stuffed the dark clothes into a machine, filled the machine with quarters, set it going, and settled down with his book, although the machinations of Russian espionage didn't hold him quite as much as they had before his encounter with Bennett.

CHAPTER 5

A SHADOW blocked the light, and he looked up to see Bennett holding up a to-go cup. "Peace offering?" Bennett looked sheepish, and the expression seemed out of place on his strong face.

Cris eyed the cup. "Is it poisoned?"

"No, but it does come with a dose of humble pie."

It was a latte. Cris sipped it as Bennett sat down with a sigh. "I figure I owe you an explanation."

"You don't owe me anything, except maybe to stop biting my head off every five minutes."

"If it's any consolation, I'm not really shouting at you, I'm shouting at myself."

"I'm just your punching bag?" Cris asked dryly.

"Something like that," Bennett agreed. "Are those my clothes?" He pointed to the machine next to Cris's.

"Yeah. I figured they were here, I may as well get them washed."

"I'm surprised you haven't set them on fire."

"I left my Zippo behind." He sipped the coffee as Bennett broke into a wry chuckle.

"Thank heaven for small mercies." Bennett paused. "There's something you have to understand—I don't care if Mikey is gay or not."

Cris raised an eyebrow. "It sure doesn't sound like it."

"I know, and...." Bennett stared at the laundry as it made an endless cycle in the machine.

"And?" Cris prompted.

"My parents. They're good people, but they're old-fashioned and don't understand being...."

Cris supplied the last word. "Gay?"

"Yeah."

Cris could have told Bennett to go away, that it wasn't his business. But he wasn't like that. If there was a problem, he wanted to fix it. If there was a chance for him to be helpful, Cris leaped in with both feet. "Tell me about your family."

"My parents are from Poland. They came here in the early eighties, and Tata—my father—found a job in construction. It turned out he had a head for business. I was born a year after they arrived." Bennett reached into his jacket and pulled out his wallet. He flipped it open to show a faded color photo of a young couple and a baby.

"This is you?"

"Yeah. My sister Hannah is three years younger than me, and Mikey came along eight years later. There was a sister in between who was stillborn."

"I'm sorry."

Bennett pressed his lips together. "I don't remember much about it. Mama and Tata went to the hospital and didn't come back with a baby. She was devastated and took a long time to recover. When Mikey came along, she focused all her attention on him." He gave a cynical smile. "Maybe too much attention."

"He was spoiled?"

"We all spoiled him. Hannah and I were just as guilty. We were so pleased he was healthy."

"My little brother's the same," Cris said, "although we've got no excuse."

"You're the oldest?"

Cris shook his head. "The middle kid, the forgotten child." He laughed as Bennett rolled his eyes.

"Yeah, yeah. Are you sure you haven't been talking to Hannah?"

"I think it's every middle child ever."

"Try being the eldest."

"You get to do everything first," Cris pointed out.

"Parents aren't as strict with the second child as they are with the first. I bet your older sibling would agree with me. Brother or sister?"

"Sister. Sally. My parents think the sun shines out of her ass. Between Sally and Jake, who are engineers, I'm the black sheep of the family. They don't approve of my lifestyle. But they can't say too much because I pay my way and don't ask them for money, unlike my little brother. He's always on the take."

Bennett looked at him curiously. "I gotta ask, why did you end up as a stripper?"

"I fell into it when I was at college. I needed a job, and my roommate suggested the club. It was good money, and after college I wanted to clear my student debt. Although that's getting harder now."

"You went to college?"

"Don't sound so surprised."

"What did you study?"

"Engineering," Cris said ruefully. "It's in the blood. My father and grandfather were civil engineers."

"You didn't want to be an engineer?"

Cris shook his head. "I knew as soon as I started that I didn't want to be an engineer, but changing courses wasn't an option, not with my family. I want to go back to school to do a fine arts course, but financing it is another matter."

"You're an artist?"

"Yeah. It's what I do when I'm not taking my clothes off for a living." Cris heard a gasp and looked up to see an elderly woman staring at him with a horrified expression on her face. He smiled at her. "It's okay, ma'am, I'm a stripper." She rushed away as though the hounds of hell were nipping at her heels, and Cris laughed softly.

"That was mean," Bennett said. "You've probably given her palpitations."

"I live to horrify elderly ladies. It's a gift."

"And all the middle-aged ones are trying to rip your clothes off?" Bennett hazarded.

Cris chuckled again. "Something like that."

Bennett was silent for a moment, and then he asked, "Do your parents know you're gay?"

"Yeah, they do. Mom wasn't happy when she found out, but only because she was worried how people would react to me. She was... amazing. If anyone gave me any trouble, she was in there, all mama bear on them. Dad was quieter, until I told them I wasn't going to be an engineer. Then he got loud, and how." Cris winced at the memory. "Apparently being a stripper is a thousand times worse than being gay. Who knew?"

Bennett snorted. "Your parents sound amazing."

"They are," Cris agreed. "My sister wasn't happy to find out I was gay, but again, I think that was just because she was worried about me. My brother couldn't care less. He's not really into relationships, male or female. He's more interested in his widgets."

"What the hell is a widget?"

Cris opened his mouth to answer but instead asked, "Do you really care?"

"Not really," Bennett admitted.

"What do you do?"

"I'm in construction, like Mikey. Our family runs a construction company out of Greenpoint."

Cris snapped his fingers. "Petrovski Construction. That's why I know your name. My father did some work with your company years ago, on the Hammond building."

"You have a good memory."

"I think my father would rather forget that building ever existed."

"My parents feel the same way about it. I think the architect must have been high when he designed it."

They both laughed over unexpected shared memories. Cris struggled to reconcile the man who insisted his brother wasn't gay with the man sitting before him, relaxed and happy to share family information. He was about to say something when Bennett suddenly looked at his watch.

"Oh hell, I really have to go. I promised Mama I'd pick her up and take her out to lunch. Is the laundry finished?"

Cris looked at Bennett's washing machine. "I'll finish your laundry. Do you want it dried?"

"You don't have to do that."

"I'm here for mine. It won't take much longer to do yours as well. I can drop it back to you, or you could pick it up from my place later on. I'm not working today, so I'll be around this evening."

"Thanks." Bennett looked sheepish again. "I spent all weekend trying to deal with Mikey, and I forgot my own chores. Let me take down your address."

He programmed it into his phone and then drew out a handful of quarters and gave them to Cris.

"I don't need this money."

"Take it anyway." Bennett's smile was warm and friendly.

Cris bit his lip and then decided to take the plunge. "I've gotta ask, Bennett. For someone who hates gays, you've been very friendly to me this morning."

"I don't hate gays." Bennett ran a hand through his hair, which left it sticking up in all directions. "I just know Mikey."

"If he's isn't gay, then he's bisexual."

"It doesn't matter what he is. My parents—"

"He can't spend his whole life hiding who he is because of your parents," Cris said gently. "He's already screwed up. You can see that, can't you?"

Bennett's expression was bleak. "Of course I can see it. Who do you think's been trying to help him all these years?"

"Making him get engaged to a woman is not helping him."

"You don't understand."

"Then help me understand, Bennett. Because from where I'm sitting, one gay son is not the end of the world. One gay son who's going to do something real stupid soon unless he gets help could *make* it the end of the world."

"My parents." Bennett held up a hand as Cris started to speak. "My parents haven't got one gay son."

"Mikey's not straight." Cris raised his voice in exasperation, and a hipster who'd been carrying on an animated conversation on his phone glowered at him.

"I know," Bennett admitted surprisingly.

"Then—?"

"Don't you get it?"

"Get what?" Cris demanded.

Bennett scrubbed through his hair. "I'm gay too. My parents have two gay sons."

"Oh fuck," Cris whispered.

"Succinct and to the point." Bennett gave him a bitter smile. "And before you ask, they don't know about me either."

"Does Mikey?"

"No, and I'm not going to tell him."

"Do you have a girlfriend?"

"I just haven't found the right girl yet." Another bitter smile. "I have to go, but I'm trusting you. If Mikey or my parents found out...."

As far as Cris could see, it would be good for Mikey to find out he had a brother like him, but now was not the time to tell Bennett. "I'll see you later."

Bennett left him more confused than ever, and Cris's book slipped to the floor forgotten as he stared unseeing at the machines. Why the hell was he getting involved with a family more screwed up than his own?

CHAPTER 6

CRIS SPENT a couple of hours at the gym. In the locker room, he nodded at a couple of guys he recognized, and they nodded back, but that was the extent of their interaction. Cris liked his gym because of the location—close to his apartment but far enough away from Forbidden Nightz that he wasn't likely to meet too many patrons of the club.

He changed into shorts and an old T-shirt, plugged in his headphones, and put on his workout playlist. Then he did his usual workout, ignoring the admiring looks that came his way from men and women. Cris knew he stood out in a crowd. His bright red hair was hard to miss.

After the weights, the rowing machine, and the cross-trainer, Cris did his usual ten-mile run on the treadmill. He appreciated the mindless monotony. It gave him a chance to think. Usually he focused on his latest painting and spent his time considering angles and perspective. He didn't paint by instinct. Before he laid one mark on the canvas, he planned the painting from start to finish. Running gave him the chance to think and plan. But today, as he pounded through the miles, his thoughts were elsewhere, tied up with a solemn-eyed, brown-haired man who seemed to have the weight of the world on his shoulders.

Cris knew he shouldn't focus on Bennett Petrovski. He was complicated, and Cris preferred his relationships simple. He didn't mind excitement, but he preferred his men to come with less baggage. There was nothing simple about Bennett, and he came with a whole set of luggage.

A young man suddenly wandered over to the window directly opposite him. Cris watched him curiously. He was dark-haired, like Bennett, but much younger. Cris suspected he'd have a whole lot fewer complications too. Their eyes caught for a moment and connected, but then the man looked over his shoulder as though someone had called him. He looked back, gave Cris the briefest of smiles, and walked away. Cris sighed and slowed the machine. He thought of Bennett again and the way he'd brought coffee to apologize for being an asshole.

Dammit, he wanted complicated.

After the gym, he moved on to the salon for his usual facial and waxing session. He didn't have much body hair, and the fine red strands that covered his chest and groin were ripped out on a regular basis by Hans the Torturer. Cris found it ironic that he spent a good deal of money on his physical appearance to make himself look great for women. As a byproduct he looked great for men too, but still, as Hans ripped off a strip of wax and Cris gasped in pain, irony was at the front of his mind.

After the workout and torture, Cris felt he was owed a burrito and a coffee, so he stuffed his face with a chicken, red peppers, and onion burrito from his favorite stand and washed it down with strong coffee as he walked to his apartment.

He left Bennett's bag of clothes by his front door and took his own into his tiny bedroom to put away in the old oak dresser his mom had given him. He preferred modern furniture, but the oak dresser was a leaving-home present from his mom, and he couldn't bring himself to part company with it. He considered moving it to his studio, but he would have to pay to get it there, so that never got further than a distant thought.

Feeling strangely restless, Cris lounged on his sofa for an hour, but the psychological thriller he was reading didn't hold his attention, even though he'd been waiting anxiously for its release. He didn't need to probe too deeply for the source of his anxiety and he worked up a rather unfair resentment toward Bennett for ruining his book.

Finally he huffed, threw his book on the sofa, and laughed at himself for being an asshole. It was time he danced out his frustration. Although they were very popular, he was bored with his current set, and he'd been promising himself for weeks he would work out new routines. He opened his closet and looked at the colorful costumes that took up the length of one wall. He had more costumes than he had jeans and T-shirts stacked on the other side.

Cris scanned the leather and hats that adorned the wall, and then he smiled. He knew just the thing to shake himself out of his funk. It had been months since he'd done his cowboy and biker routines. He didn't need to buy anything new, and he quickly found the items he needed—zip-up brown leather pants, cowboy boots and hat, and a plain white, form-fitting T-shirt for the cowboy, and identical black leather pants, biker boots, and leather jacket for the biker. And the essential jockstrap. He had hundreds of them. Dancers like Raymond managed to tease the women for hours just taking off their clothes, but Cris wasn't that coordinated and got all tangled in the fabric. He did his teasing with his come-hither attitude and a few props.

Cowboy or biker first? Cris hovered his hand over the costumes. Biker it was. He stripped off his jeans and shirt, zipped up the black leather pants, and stomped into the boots. The biker boots were well-worn from hours of dancing, but they fit like a glove. He spent a fortune on good boots.

All the music he needed was on his phone. Cris scrolled through a few tracks and smiled when he found the one he wanted. Yeah, he could start off with "Highway to Hell." It had been that sort of week. He pushed back the sofa and the coffee table, pressed the button to start the music, and pumped his fist up into the air. Oh yeah, that was just what he needed. "Highway to Hell" led into "November Rain," and Cris was lost in a world of his own as he pounded out his frustrations. He was almost at the end of his biker routine when the doorbell rang. Startled, Cris looked at the clock. He hadn't expected Bennett for a couple of hours, but he jogged over and opened the door.

Bennett's smile faded as he took in Cris's state of undress. "I...."

Cris suddenly realized he'd opened the door wearing nothing but a red jockstrap and biker boots. "Oh hell, hold on." He jogged back to his bedroom and shrugged on his navy toweling robe. Back at the door, he smiled at Bennett. "I'm sorry. I was practicing my routines. I kinda forgot...." He waved at himself.

"So you don't always answer the door dressed like that?"

Cris sighed at the accusing tone. Whatever goodwill had been kindled between them earlier seemed to have vanished. "You saw me dressed like this at the club. I'm sorry if my skin offends you."

He picked up the bag of laundry by the front door and handed it to Bennett. "Here are your clothes. Goodbye."

He tried to shut the door, but Bennett held out a hand to stop him. Short of breaking the guy's hand, there was little Cris could do except wait for Bennett to get whatever it was off his chest.

Bennett huffed but then gave a rueful grin. "I'm being an ass again, aren't I?"

"Yeah. And I'm not in the mood for another Petrovski lecture."

"I'm sorry. Mikey and Julianne had a huge fight in front of my parents. I think Mikey was on the point of telling them."

"Good," Cris said shortly. "It's about time."

Bennett pressed his lips together, and Cris expected an outburst. Instead Bennett merely asked, "Are you always so blunt?"

"When it needs to be said." Because God knew, someone had to tell this family they were screwing up.

"It's none of your business," Bennett snapped.

"You boys keep dragging me into your family affairs, and I've had enough. Tell your parents, don't tell your parents, I don't care. As you said, it's not my business." Cris went to shut the door again, but once more Bennett stopped him.

"Goodbye," Cris said firmly.

Bennett stayed where he was with one hand on the door. "You don't understand. It's not as—"

Cris growled under his breath. "If that sentence is going to end with 'easy as all that,' I'm going to thump you on the nose. We've had this conversation already. Let go of my door before I break your hand."

Bennett barked out a laugh. "Everyone tells me you're the warm friendly one. Except to me."

"Everyone else isn't getting me involved in their family life." Cris gave up trying to shut his front door. He turned his back, walked away, and left Bennett standing there. If Bennett wanted to come in, that was up to him. Cris didn't care one way or the other, or at least that's what he told himself. He headed over to his fridge and pulled out a couple of bottles. When he heard the snick of the front door closing, he popped the tops off both beers and offered one to Bennett, who had followed as far as the sofa. "Beer?"

Bennett hesitated but walked over to Cris. "Thanks. Uh… are you gonna stay in that…?"

Cris looked down at his robe. "Does it bother you?"

"Some," Bennett admitted. "I'm not used to being around half-naked guys, except in the gym."

It would have been easy to make a sarcastic comment, but Bennett had been honest. Cris placed his beer bottle on the counter.

"Take a seat. I'll go change."

It took a moment to pull on the jeans and shirt from earlier, but Bennett visibly relaxed as Cris came back into the room. He was like a wire pulled so tight he was ready to snap. The only difference between him and Mikey, it seemed, was that Bennett wasn't pretending he wanted to get married.

Cris grabbed his bottle and sat at the other end of the sofa. It was the only seating in the whole place, so Bennett could suck it up or leave. There was a long, awkward silence, and then Bennett spoke.

"You're in good shape. Do you go to the gym every day?"

Cris appreciated it for the attempt to find a neutral subject. "Most days. Dancing keeps me in shape, but I like working out at the gym. It gives me a chance to think. What about you?"

"I get to the gym enough to justify my membership, but that's about all. It didn't matter so much when I was doing more of the physical work, but now I'm stuck in an office.…" He patted his stomach, and Cris couldn't help but look.

"It doesn't show," Cris assured him.

Bennett's lips twitched. So the man did have a sense of humor after all. "Thanks."

"You're welcome. You know all about my job. Tell me about yours."

"Tata—Dad—wants to retire, and he wants his sons to take over running the company. Since I left college, I've been working my way through all the departments, learning how the company operates. Mikey's more interested in the remodeling side of the work. I don't think he's much interested in the business side of the operations, but he's just amazing with his hands. He's made some furniture that he's sold for a lot of money, and he's had some stores interested in selling his work."

Cris frowned. Mikey again. It seemed that Bennett had subsumed his wants and needs into taking care of his brother. Cris liked Mikey, but he wanted to know about the man in front of him. "Do you like taking care of business?"

Bennett gave him a genuine smile. It lit up his face and made him look years younger. Cris couldn't look away. "I do. I know I'm lucky because I'm going to inherit a successful business, but Tata got us working even when we were still at school. I don't think there's a department I haven't worked in. I know how every element of our buildings come together, from purchasing the land to selling the end result."

"What did you study in college?" Cris asked curiously.

"Architecture and design. Tata wanted me to do something more hands-on, but I always knew I wanted to design buildings."

"But you don't want to be an architect now?"

Bennett shrugged. "I had to make a decision—the business or becoming an architect. I chose the business."

Or did someone choose for him? Cris didn't say it out loud, but he suspected the family had a big influence in his decision. He looked down at his empty beer bottle. He didn't have anywhere else to be, so he waved the bottle at Bennett. "Another beer?"

Bennett shook his head, somewhat regretfully. "I've got to drive home. Coffee would be great if you have it."

Cris got up to make the coffee. He was measuring out the grounds when he heard a strangled noise behind him and he turned to see Bennett staring into a corner. "You okay over there?"

"Is that a pole?" Bennett's voice cracked.

"Yep." Cris didn't bother to look at the metal pole he'd installed in one corner of the room.

"You're a pole dancer?" Bennett sounded strangled and slightly breathless.

"I'm a stripper," Cris said calmly, "but I sometimes use a pole as part of my routine."

Then Bennett surprised the hell out of Cris. "I tried to learn to pole dance when I was in college. They were offering classes to anyone who wanted to try. I was hopeless. I've got two left feet, but I gained a whole new respect for pole dancers."

"Maybe I could teach you," Cris suggested as he switched on the coffee maker.

Bennett chuckled. "As I said, I've got two left feet... and two right ones."

"That bad, huh?"

"Worse. I nearly knocked out my teacher and another student. They didn't exactly ask me to leave, but I got the picture."

"I could show you." Cris had a sudden desire to show him what he could do.

"Go ahead, then." From a man worried about jockstraps to an interest in pole dancing, once again, Bennett was a maze of contradictions.

Cris flashed him a smile, loped over to the pole, jumped and climbed up hand-over-hand in one smooth movement, only using his feet when he got to the top so he could salute Bennett, who stared at him wide-eyed. Cris smiled and swayed down the pole so he could turn upside down. He heard Bennett gasp. There wasn't enough room for some of his favorite maneuvers, but he went through a routine and felt the strain in his arms and shoulders. He wanted Bennett to admire him, but he finally lowered himself to the floor when his coffee maker beeped.

"That was.... I... you're amazing." Bennett sounded completely genuine.

Cris swept a bow and beamed at him. "I was just showing off."

"I've seen women pole dance, but it never affected me like this." Bennett let out an unexpected raucous whistle.

Cris couldn't help the immediate sweep down to check... and sure enough, the bulge told him Bennett was more than a little affected. He looked up, and Bennett bit his lip.

"Uh... coffee," Cris said. "Creamer? Sugar?"

"Uh, thanks," Bennett said hurriedly.

So maybe they were both affected, because Cris only had to look into Bennett's intense eyes and he found it hard to breathe. He focused on making the coffee before he made a complete idiot of himself, and he managed not to spill the creamer or the coffee despite his shaking hands.

They retreated to the sofa with their coffee. The last thing he needed was to lose control in front of Bennett. Silence reigned for several moments, and Cris searched for something to say that wasn't, "Wanna make out?" Because, yes, he did.

"You have a lot of DVDs and CDs," Bennett said finally as he eyed the shelves that stretched along one wall.

That was safe. Cris could answer that one. "I know. Too many. I used to be an addict when I was a student. I keep meaning to go through them and thin out the shelves. But I pick one up to start, and before I know it, I've put it in the DVD player, and I'm watching a pile of them. The family doesn't help my addiction. I get all their castoffs, and I keep them even if I don't like their taste in movies."

"I collect vinyl," Bennett confessed. "I've got more vinyl than shelving space."

"Another hoarder."

They smiled at each other.

"I keep saying I'm gonna stop," Bennett said, "and then I find another one I haven't got, and all my good intentions go up in smoke."

They grinned at each other again, and Cris thought that Bennett looked gorgeous with the crinkles around his eyes. He needed to move closer to Bennett, but before he could speak, Bennett rushed in.

"So, you're a movie addict?"

Cris sighed and settled back into his corner. "If it's made, I watch it."

"All movies?" Bennett flashed him a skeptical look.

"Pretty much."

"There's got to be one genre you don't like. What about rom-coms?"

"Love 'em." Cris had every Sandra Bullock movie in existence, and he didn't care who knew it.

"Kids' movies."

"Got them all."

"Marvel or DC?"

Cris raised an eyebrow. "Have you seen the bottom shelf?"

Bennett held up his hands in horror. "Oh dear God, you're a monster. You're definitely worse than me. At least I only collect what I like. I'm going to need more coffee to deal with this."

Cris waved at the coffeepot. "Help yourself. You can go check the shelves out."

Bennett heaved himself to his feet, poured more coffee, and did as he was told. "You're worse than Blockbusters."

Cris chuckled. "I told you. It's an addiction."

Bennett turned to him, his eyes comically wide. "Oh my God, you even have—"

"Yes, I have that too. The whole series." Cris knew exactly what Bennett had discovered.

"But—"

"My sister bought it as a joke." She'd been so sure Cris wouldn't watch them, she'd bet him $100.

"Did you watch it?"

"Of course. I've watched them all." *Fifty Shades of Grey* was in his collection.

CHAPTER 7

A SUDDEN shiver penetrated Cris's comfortable sleep. Before he even opened his eyes he was aware he was cold—really cold. Cris raised his head and looked around. The TV showed the DVD menu and played the menu music on repeat. No, they hadn't watched anything with love or het sex in it. Bennett confessed to a liking for sci-fi, so *The Martian* it was. Still drowsy, Cris sat up and yawned. He must have fallen asleep during the movie. He looked around, intending to apologize to Bennett, only to find him curled up in the corner, his mouth open, letting out a snore on every other breath. Cris contemplated snapping a picture with his phone, but he didn't know Bennett well enough to play that sort of prank.

He squinted at his phone. 2:47 a.m. Christ, when had they fallen asleep? He remembered finishing the pizza, and then they had another beer, but after that, it was a blur. Cris suspected he hadn't stayed awake much past the opening credits.

Bennett snored again. He could wake him, but Bennett looked relaxed and comfortable. Cris wondered how many evenings he got to chill out without work or family distractions. He grabbed the thick furry throw and his grandma's quilt from the back of the sofa and covered Bennett, who grumbled and snuggled under the blankets without waking. Cris turned off the TV and DVD player and staggered to bed via the bathroom. He didn't bother to undress and was asleep before he'd fully woken up.

The second time he woke up in the morning, he wasn't sure what had disturbed him. He was just aware something was different. He shuffled out of his bedroom to find Bennett sitting up, the throw pooling around his waist and the quilt on the floor. He blinked like a startled owl and looked more than a little sheepish.

"I'm sorry. I must have fallen asleep." Bennett yawned, and his jaw cracked. "You should have thrown me out."

"We both slept. You looked comfortable, so I left you there. Coffee?" Cris waved the coffeepot.

"How about breakfast?" Bennett offered as he stood and rolled his shoulders. "My treat for doing my laundry yesterday."

"Aren't you due at work?"

Bennett grimaced. "Dad made me take a couple of vacation days. He says I'm working too hard. Anyway, breakfast?"

Cris smiled. "Yeah, definitely. I'm starving. Do you want a shower?"

"I'll go home and shower after we've eaten." Bennett rubbed his dark stubble. "I'll have to shave before I go back to work tomorrow. Tata doesn't approve of businessmen with beards. He says it looks untidy."

Cris thought the tousled and unshaven look on Bennett looked damn sexy, and from the fluttery feeling in his stomach, the rest of him agreed. "You look fine."

Bennett flushed under his regard. "So do you."

Cris rubbed his chin and felt the growth. His ginger stubble wasn't nearly as sexy as Bennett's but if the man liked it, who was he to disagree? He had the sudden mental image of listening to Bennett groan as he dragged his chin up and down Bennett's sensitized skin. He put away that thought hastily and then caught Bennett staring at him as though he could read Cris's thoughts.

They shared a heated look, and Cris was on the verge of dropping to his knees when Bennett's stomach rumbled. Then Cris coughed, laughed, and turned away to look for his boots. As Cris laced them up, the fluttery feeling in the pit of his stomach continued. Bennett was goddamn more than fine. He pushed all of Cris's buttons. Cris could make a real fool of himself over Bennett if he wasn't careful.

Bennett refused to look directly at him when Cris raised his head again. They shrugged into their coats and scarves, and Bennett waited patiently for Cris to find his gloves.

"You should sew your gloves onto elastic and thread them through your coat," Bennett suggested.

"My nana used to do that," Cris admitted. "I think I was twelve before she stopped giving me mittens on elastic every winter."

Bennett chuckled as they left the apartment. "Nanas know best."

"You try going to school with mittens on elastic in the seventh grade," Cris retorted.

"The kids gave you hell?"

"Between the ginger hair, the braces, and the mittens?"

Bennett winced in sympathy. "You poor thing."

Cris grunted. That was an era he never wanted to repeat.

IN THE overheated diner, they shed their hats, gloves, scarves, and coats and settled into a booth and waited for the waitress to pour coffee. On principle Cris ignored Bennett's admonishment to put his gloves in his coat pockets. Then he rubbed his eyes and yawned. He wasn't used to being up early in the morning. Bennett, on the other hand, was bright-eyed and way too cheerful for Cris's liking.

"I'm always up early," Bennett said when Cris grouched about his cheerfulness. "By the time you go to bed, I'm about ready to wake up."

"You're a monster," Cris grumbled.

Bennett looked at him over the rim of his cup. "Are you always this grumpy in the morning?"

"I don't do mornings or midday, or anything that involves having to be cheerful and talk to people."

"So I've noticed," Bennett said, his tone mild. Cris had the feeling he was laughing at him. "What do you usually do on your days off?"

"If I'm not working, I'm painting. I share studio space in Dumbo."

"I remember. Is it possible to see your paintings?"

Cris groaned at the look of expectation on Bennett's face. "Okay, but you're not allowed to be shocked."

"Shocked? You mean like when you opened the door to me in a jockstrap, or when I discovered a pole in your room? You mean that type of shocked?"

The grin on Bennett's face reassured Cris that he was mocking himself as much as Cris.

"Yeah. That type of shocked."

"Just what is it you paint, Mr. Peters?" Bennett obviously wasn't going to let it go.

"The male form." Among other things, but Cris started with the one that would more likely shock a Petrovski.

Bennett's eyebrow shot up. "You mean nudes?"

"Some. Not always," Cris corrected. "Just always men."

"Would you show me?"

Cris blinked at him. "Now?"

"You can finish your pancakes first."

"Thanks," Cris said drily and stuffed a pancake in his mouth before Bennett changed his mind.

WHEN THEY left the diner, Cris almost left his gloves behind, and he could feel Bennett's smirk burning into his back all the way out to the sidewalk. Cris ignored him with the expertise of years of ignoring a bossy older sibling.

He was nervous as they made their way to Cris's studio, and his stomach churned, although he tried not to show it. Plenty of people had seen his work over the years, but never a man who he was attracted to like this. Bennett's opinion counted, and that annoyed him.

He shoved his hands in his pockets to hide the fact they were shaking as Bennett stared at the huge canvases leaning against the wall. Bennett had said nothing, but murmured softly, which made Cris more nervous as he waited for Bennett to say something—anything.

Finally Bennett turned to him, his eyes wide, and Cris licked his lips nervously.

"My God, Cris, these are amazing."

Relieved beyond measure, Cris nodded so fast he felt like the bobblehead dog his aunt used to have in her car. His latest paintings were outstanding. He knew that. He'd taken a different approach and painted a series of buildings in the stages of construction. In each one he'd focused on one man working on the building.

"This is one of our buildings." Bennett pointed at a shell of a structure and a man, covered in brick dust, his arm muscles bulging as he pushed a wheelbarrow.

"Probably several of them are. I constantly hunt for new sites and take photos." Cris drew Bennett to one corner of the studio. He was lucky. Because he and friends leased the space privately, he could keep all his equipment there. "I have folders of photos of the city."

"You don't take digital photos?"

"I do, but I prefer something physical to look at. I'm tactile. I need to pick up something and look at it."

Cris opened one of the folders to show Bennett hundreds of photos of the partially constructed building from all angles. "It takes me a long time to decide how I'm going to paint the building. I plan it from beginning to end."

Bennett traced the lines of the building. "You're still an engineer at heart." Cris opened his mouth to disagree, but Bennett continued. "Tata would love to see these. I think he's more excited about the design and construction of the building than he is the end result."

"I can understand that. My dad's like that too." Cris was the same about his painting. He was always proud of a finished painting, but the planning was the thing that excited him.

"You have a real talent," Bennett murmured.

"Thanks." Cris closed the folder of photos and put it away. "Now I've just got to get ready for my exhibition."

"I can't wait to see them hanging in a gallery." Bennett slowly looked at each painting again and shook his head. "You should be doing this for a living."

Cris laughed. "All artists want to be painting full-time. But we know that's probably a pipe dream."

Bennett sighed. "It's like my dream of becoming an architect— maybe one day."

Cris slid the folder back onto the shelf. He wanted to challenge Bennett on his comment about being an architect. But he didn't want to ruin the peace between them. "I'm gonna spend some time here before I get ready for work. Do you want a coffee before you leave?"

Bennett hesitated and then shook his head. "I should get home. But thanks for showing me your art."

"You're welcome."

He showed Bennett to the door, but as Bennett went to leave, Cris said, "How would you feel about me painting you?"

Bennett blinked and blinked again. "You want to paint me?" He sounded shocked like the mere thought was outlandish.

But Cris nodded. "I'd like to see you holding plans by one of your buildings."

"Not naked?" Bennett asked suspiciously.

Cris couldn't help the twitch of his lips. "If you want to be naked, I'd be more than happy to—"

Bennett shook his head vehemently. "No, no, that's fine."

"If you're sure…."

"I'm sure." Bennett gave a wry grin. "No one's ever wanted to paint me before. I'm not really a model."

Cris took Bennett by the shoulders and swiveled him around to look at the paintings again. "The guys in this series aren't models. They're workmen doing their jobs. I'm not interested in stylized models. For these paintings I wanted blue-collar guys doing their jobs. Although I paint models and dancers too." He led Bennett over to another series of paintings. Cris was in the middle of a series of male dancers and hoped to show them when the group was finished. He'd spent hours watching a male troupe practice. He focused on the play of their muscles across their backs and legs. "I paint all kinds of men. Look at the musculature on these dancers. Those guys are all muscle. They have to be, with the lifts and moves they do."

"You remind me of them," Bennett said suddenly. "When I saw you use the pole yesterday, I thought how graceful but strong you looked. I've never seen anyone use the pole like that."

"Thanks." Cris patted his shoulder. "It's a good workout."

"Do you really want to paint me? Wouldn't Mikey be more your style?"

Cris growled, frustrated by the mention of Mikey yet again. "No. You're the one I want to paint."

"Uh, okay. When and where?"

"How about starting now? I need to take photos of you first." Cris was excited again at the thought of a new project.

"Now?" Bennett looked startled.

"Unless you're busy." Cris left it there. He didn't want to pressure Bennett. The last thing Bennett needed was added stress.

"I guess not." Bennett sounded like he wanted to bolt, so Cris beamed at him.

"I'm gonna make us coffee, and then we'll get started."

"I'm so gonna regret this, aren't I?"

Bennett scrubbed a hand through his hair, sending the curls every which way. Cris stepped forward and gently combed the thick hair back into a neat shape. As he pushed the last lock into place, Cris became aware that Bennett was holding his breath, so he bent down and brushed Bennett's soft mouth with his. Bennett growled against his lips and hauled him closer, his mouth opening under Cris's, demanding more than a teasing kiss. Cris obliged, and the kiss turned deep and passionate. They pushed their hands through each other's hair, and Cris disturbed Bennett's curls again. After a long while their kissing gentled to something more tender, and they relaxed their clutching hands as they took one last kiss.

Cris buried his face in Bennett's neck and inhaled his musky scent. Yeah, he needed a shower, but he smelled male... exciting. "You smell so good," he murmured.

"So do you," Bennett said as he steered Cris against the wall. They kissed again, and the part of Cris's brain that was still south of his navel was amazed at Bennett's enthusiasm. He seemed to have no fear of touching Cris.

They entwined their fingers, and they rubbed against each other, arousal pressing against arousal. Bennett rubbed his palm over Cris's erection and squeezed gently.

Cris groaned and pressed into his hand. "You're driving me crazy."

"Likewise," Bennett gasped. "Can I?" Bennett rested his forehead against Cris's and placed a hand on his waistband.

"Oh yeah." At that point Bennett could do whatever he wanted.

He sucked in his stomach as Bennett gently undid the button and slowly pulled the zipper down. Cris didn't breathe as he waited for the instant Bennett reached in to press his hand against his damp briefs. He closed his eyes at the exquisite feel of Bennett's sure touch.

"All right?" Bennett breathed in his ear.

"Touch me," Cris demanded.

Bennett did as he was told and wrapped his warm hand around Cris's cock. Cris groaned, and scrabbled at Bennett's waistband, needing to feel him, to touch him in exactly the same way he was being touched. Bennett stilled his hand and seemed to wait in that same breathless anticipation that Cris felt.

Cris grazed Bennett's furry belly with his knuckles and looked down. The head of Bennett's cock poked above the waistband of his dark green briefs. Fixing Bennett with his gaze, Cris licked the pad of his thumb and gently swiped it over the head and dipped into the slit and around again.

Bennett groaned. "Do that again."

Cris did, then he slipped his hand into Bennett's briefs to cup the soft sacs below. Bennett did the same to him, and they stood for a moment, panting into each other's ears.

Then Bennett wrapped his hand around Cris's cock and slowly jacked him, and the feeling was so deep that Cris almost raised up on his toes to go with it.

"Do the same to me," Bennett begged, and Cris pushed down Bennett's briefs because he needed more room to hold the thick shaft.

Cris rested against the wall, and Bennett pressed against him as they slowly tugged each other to climax. They kissed too, their soft murmurs of pleasure captured between heated kisses. Bennett was a skilled kisser, and he eagerly explored Cris's mouth with his tongue. But as they drove each other to orgasm, the kisses became more of a panting against mouths, the groans louder, words incoherent. Bennett slid his free hand around the back of Cris's neck and held him tighter while Cris jacked Bennett's dick faster and felt the sticky precome around the ring of his fingers. He relished Bennett's groan against his mouth as his thigh muscles started to shake. He wanted them to come together, but he didn't know how much longer he could hold on. Then Bennett thrust up through his fingers, yelled his completion, and hot, sticky fluid covered Bennett's hand. Cris's orgasm was a heartbeat later in the lax channel that was Bennett's grip.

Bennett rested against him for long moments and then took a step back. He looked at the mess in his hand and laughed. "We've got to clean up."

Cris was still coasting the afterglow of an orgasm and took a moment to catch up. "Hmm." Then his brain clicked into place. "Wait here." He pushed off the wall, went back to the desk, and returned with a large industrial-size roll of tissue paper. He handed a couple of sheets to Bennett. "Use this first. The bathroom's just down the hall."

Bennett took the tissue and wiped his hands. Cris did the same and bent down to mop the floor between them.

Bennett laughed as he rubbed at the hair on his belly. "I really need that shower now. Maybe the coffee and photos will have to wait until another day?"

Cris nodded regretfully, but Bennett was right. His mind was blown, even after a simple hand job. It wasn't the time to plan another painting and take photos. He also had to admit there was nothing simple about that hand job. "I'll walk you out."

Which he did, via the bathroom, where they attempted to clean up a little better. With a grunt of disgust, Bennett threw the paper towel in the trashcan. "I'm leaving before I make my clothes even wetter."

Cris agreed with him, gave up on the cleanup, and walked Bennett to the huge door that led outside. They stood facing each other, and Cris sought for something to say. "Thank you. That was...."

"Unexpected?" Bennett suggested.

"Amazing," Cris said.

"And that." Bennett leaned forward as though he had every intention of kissing Cris, but then his expression changed. "Dammit."

"What?"

"I left my laundry at your place."

Cris grinned. "Now you have an excuse to come visit me again."

From the conflicted expression on Bennett's face as he left, the idea both terrified and delighted him.

CHAPTER 8

THE BACK door to Forbidden Nightz was locked, as usual. It was too early for the club to be open for customers, and the doorbell was a tinny, useless affair that the manager kept meaning to deal with, but somehow never did. Cris leaned on the button, knowing it would take a long time to attract the manager's attention. He was about to start banging on the door when he heard heavy footsteps thunder down the stairs, and finally the door flung open.

Marlon, the manager, scowled at him. He was a short, stocky man dressed in a too-tight T-shirt and saggy jeans. An ex-stripper, Marlon was tubby around the middle, and his once-thick head of blond hair had thinned on top into a comb-over. "Cris? What are you doing here?"

"It's Friday. I work on Friday, remember?" Cris said.

Marlon shook his head. "That's not right."

He thundered back up the stairs, and Cris followed. With a sinking feeling in the pit of his stomach, he let the door swing shut behind him. They headed into the office, where Marlon stabbed at the keyboard on the messy desk. The screen sprang into life, and Cris waited while Marlon brought up the roster.

Marlon pointed to the green blob that represented Fridays on the roster. "Oh yeah, see? Ray's doing tonight. And the new guy, Olly. I swapped you over to Saturday. I told you last week."

"No, you didn't," Cris said, gripping so tightly on to his bag that he dug his nails in his palm. "If you had, I'd have told you I can't do another Saturday. Friday is my night. It's always been my night. Can't Olly do Saturday?"

Marlon shook his head. "I'm training him. I need to be around, so it has to be Friday, not Saturday. It's a big party tomorrow night, and we need Lionman. You know I wouldn't book you in if I didn't think you could handle them."

"That's not the point. You keep changing my days." Cris was angry. He was sick and tired of being fucked around.

"A couple of times. Jeez." From the way Marlon was huffing, you'd have thought he was the one being screwed over.

"Come on, Marlon, this is the fourth time you've changed the rosters and not told me. Enough is enough."

Marlon's face hardened. "I'm the manager, and you'll do what I tell you. If I say you're working Saturdays, then you're working Saturdays."

Cris straightened up and returned the scowl with one of his own. "I thought I was your star act. The Lionman. Lionman picks his own hours. Isn't that what you told me?"

Marlon shrugged. "That was then. You're older now. New kids like Olly are coming in."

Cris gritted his teeth. Olly was barely wet behind the ears. He could dance, but he knew nothing about wooing a crowd.

"I'm twenty-five, not fifty-five." It was mean of Cris, but the age jab was deliberate. Marlon would be fifty-five next year.

Judging by Marlon's angry expression, it struck home. "Take it or leave it, kid. You're a stripper, not a headliner."

Cris stared at him in disbelief, because he was the headliner. "If I leave it?"

"Clear your locker out and don't bother coming back."

"You've got to be joking."

"Do I look like I'm laughing?"

What the hell? Cris had gone from golden balls to donkey balls in the space of a week?

"I'll get my stuff from the locker," he muttered.

Marlon looked as shocked as Cris felt, but he just nodded. Cris turned to leave, only to have his path blocked by a young black man.

"Olly."

"Hey, Lionman." Olly saluted him. "I thought you were on tomorrow."

Cris gave him a tight smile. "Not now, kiddo. See you around."

He pushed past the bewildered young man and headed to the dressing room where they kept the lockers. Technically they were for everyone, but some of the longer-standing dancers had claimed them as their own. He fumbled with the padlock until the numbers were in the right combination and finally managed to open it. He put the padlock in his bag and shoved the contents of the locker—mainly costumes and toiletries—on top.

"Cris?" Olly seemed uncertain of his reception.

Cris smiled at him, trying to be reassuring. "It's okay, Olly. Really."

Olly didn't smile back. "It's not, though, is it? Marlon says he's fired you."

He would say that, wouldn't he? Asshole. "Yeah, kind of. Maybe it's time I moved on and allowed fresh blood in."

"But you're Lionman. You're the headline act." Olly sounded shocked.

"There's always time for a change." Cris zippered up the bag. "Listen to what everyone tells you, and you'll be a great act."

"But I was learning from you."

Cris hadn't even realized Olly had been watching him. "I gotta go. Look after yourself, Olly. You'll do fine." He heaved the bag on his shoulder. "I'll be okay."

He patted Olly's back and walked out. As Cris ran down the stairs, he heard Olly call after him, but he ignored him, slammed his hand on the door and pushing through the second he heard the lock click.

The steady downfall of cold rain quickly soaked through Cris's jacket, and he called an Uber. He gave the address of Cowboys and Angels, knowing there was a good chance Bennett would be there. Bennett had said that's where he'd be as Cris was working. Cris snorted. *Supposed* to be working. Now all he could think of through the white noise in his head was, get to Bennett and everything would be okay.

It was happy hour at Cowboys and Angels, and the place was heaving. Not seeing Bennett and definitely not up to facing a large crowd, Cris stood in the doorway. He was on the point of leaving when someone pushed him inside from behind.

"Hurry up, man, it's freezing out here."

Cris stumbled but recovered his balance as he glared at the man. "Watch it," he snapped.

The guy, a tall Latino with beautiful eyes—yes, Cris noticed that, even as he glared at him—scowled back. Then he was hailed by someone else and veered off in their direction. Cris huffed and headed to the bar, where he waited for Dan to finish with the customer in front.

Dan studied him closely. "Hey, you look like crap."

"Thanks," Cris said with a wry smile. "Is Bennett or Mikey here?"

"Not yet. Weren't you supposed to be working tonight?"

"Not according to my ex-manager."

Of course Dan picked the wording up immediately. "Ex?"

"Marlon fired me. I walked out. Take your pick."

Dan looked at Ariel, who was chatting to friends at one end of the bar. "Hey, minion. Can you take over for a moment? Got a crisis here."

"I'm not a crisis," Cris protested as Ariel came over.

Dan ignored him. "Just gonna take Cris up to the apartment. If Bennett comes in, send him up."

"I'm supposed to be done for the day," she said.

"I'll be fifteen minutes. Then you'll be finished."

"That's what you said two hours ago," Ariel pointed out, but she didn't seem too annoyed.

"You should've gone when you had the chance."

Ariel flipped him off, but she smiled at the next customer. "What can I get you?"

Dan pointed a finger at the stairs to Gideon's apartment above the bar. "I'll meet you there."

Cris made his way through the throng and waited for Dan at the foot of the stairs.

Dan opened the door and gestured to Cris to go upstairs. "Gideon's out this evening. Some business thing. He had to dress up, and he bitched all afternoon."

"He won't mind me going upstairs?" Cris asked as Dan led the way.

Dan snorted. "It's his apartment, not a palace. You'll be lucky if you can find anywhere to sit."

Dan wasn't kidding. The whole place was covered in clothes, and unless Gideon had started dressing in skimpy dresses, Ariel used the place as her personal closet. Cris gingerly pushed a couple of items to one side.

"They won't bite, dude. Anyway, you must be used to touching women's clothing."

"That makes me sound like some kind of pervert," Cris pointed out.

"You have the job of many men's dreams. Those guys down there would kill to have women screaming for them."

Cris pulled a face. "Had the job. Now I'm unemployed, and unless I find something soon, also homeless."

"Tell me what happened." Dan pulled up a dining chair, swung it around, and straddled the seat. He leaned his arms against the back and waited for Cris to explain.

"Marlon fucked up the schedule. Only he hasn't been fucking up the schedule."

Dan raised an eyebrow. "Go on."

"He's got new dancers, younger guys. He wants to train them."

"What's that got to do with the schedule?"

"He thinks the club could do with fresh blood. I'm an old hand." Cris tried to keep the bitterness out of his tone, but from the look on Dan's face, he wasn't very successful.

"I'm still confused. He's messing up the schedules while he trains new guys to replace you?"

"Something like that."

"But you're the top act."

"I'm twenty-five. They're nineteen. In stripper years I'm ancient."

"Bullshit," Dan said. "I've seen those shows. The guys are working well after twenty-five."

"Not according to Marlon."

"So he fired you?"

"Uh, I think I walked out, but I'm not really sure. The upshot is I don't have a job anymore."

"You've got a job here as long as you need it," Dan said without a moment's hesitation. "But other clubs would kill to have you. You're the Lionman. I've seen you in action—kinda. You need to start asking around."

"Thanks," Cris said, relieved that one worry was off his plate. "My rent's due soon. I can pay it, but it doesn't leave a lot to live on."

"Take shifts here. I'm looking for extra staff. You working here gives me a break too."

"Thanks. I won't let you down."

"You haven't so far. But give yourself a breather before you start looking for a new club."

"I could do with a break," Cris admitted.

"Uh... hello?"

Cris turned to see Bennett in the doorway with a worried expression on his face. "Hey."

"Ariel sent me up here. Said you might be in need of a shoulder?"

Dan got to his feet. "That's my cue to leave. Be here tomorrow at ten. It's a long day. Don't wear high heels."

"Very funny," Cris said sourly.

"I thought so. Okay. I'll see you downstairs."

Dan vanished down the stairs, and Bennett looked confused. "What's happened? I thought you were working tonight?"

"To cut a long story short, I'm no longer a stripper at Forbidden Nightz. Dan has offered me a bar job here temporarily."

Cris expected questions. What he got was Bennett wrapping him in his arms. Cris buried his face in the crook of Bennett's neck and inhaled the clean scent of him. Bennett stroked Cris's hair, and Cris shuddered and relaxed into him.

"It's okay. Shhh, it's okay."

Bennett murmured the words over and over, and after a while, Cris began to believe him. He was okay. He had a job, he had time to plan, and being in Bennett's arms was really, really nice. They breathed in sync for a while, and it was soothing. When he raised his head, Bennett loosened his embrace just enough to allow some space between them.

"Thanks," Cris murmured.

Bennett stroked gentle fingers down his cheek. "Whenever you need me."

Cris needed him then. He just wanted to bury his face in Bennett's neck and stay there all evening. But he forced himself not to fall apart. "Likewise."

"Do you want to talk about what happened?" Bennett asked.

The last thing Cris wanted to do was discuss it all over again, but he owed Bennett the truth. "Buy me a beer and a whiskey chaser, and I'll tell you anything you want to know."

"You can't get too drunk. You've got to work tomorrow."

Cris pulled a face. "Thanks for reminding me. I never get up before noon on a Saturday."

"You poor boy." Bennett patted Cris's ass.

"Now you're making fun of me."

"What gave it away?"

"Girl in the house," Ariel yelled up the stairs.

Cris grinned at Bennett. "You can come up. We're both dressed."

She appeared in the room, a shit-eating grin on her face. "Now if I were a different kind of girl, I'd make a smart-aleck remark about that. But I'm not, so I'll just say get your asses downstairs. I want to change."

"You are the queen of smart-aleck remarks," Bennett informed her, "but I don't want to scar my boyfriend for life, so I'll take him downstairs."

Boyfriend? Cris stopped breathing. Bennett just called him his boyfriend. When did that happen?

Unaware of Cris's mental freak-out, Ariel rolled her eyes. "You have met your boyfriend, haven't you? He's had more half-naked women in his hands than most men get in a lifetime."

"Thanks," Cris muttered. "Now he's gonna think I'm easy."

Bennett dropped a kiss on his cheek. "No, you're the last person I'd think that about."

"Get out of here before I melt from the sugary sweetness." Ariel shooed them to the top of the stairs. "What is it about you men? All hard-core until you fall in love, and then you get all sappy."

Love? Who said anything about love? Cris hadn't gotten over the boyfriend issue yet. From the freaked look on Bennett's face, he was thinking the same thing.

"Ariel's always getting ahead of herself," he murmured as he picked up his bag and started down the stairs.

"Wait," Bennett said.

Cris turned to look up at him. "Yeah?"

"The boyfriend comment—"

"It was just a spur of the moment thing. I get it."

Bennett nodded, his expression uncertain.

"I kinda like the idea at some point, though," Cris admitted. "When you're ready."

"I think.... Me too. At some point."

They smiled at each other, and Cris turned to go down the stairs.

Cowboys and Angels seemed more crowded than usual. Cris headed to the bar, but Bennett grabbed his arm and steered him to the door.

On the sidewalk Bennett said, "It's packed in there, and I'd like to have you to myself for a while. Have you eaten?"

Cris's stomach rumbled in response, the sound loud in the relative quiet outside the bar.

"I guess that's your answer. I was gonna eat after work."

"I know a great Thai restaurant near where I live. Do you like Thai food?"

"Yeah, I do."

"It's a hole-in-the-wall place, but the food is great." Bennett looked nervous, as though he expected to be rejected.

"That would be great," Cris said promptly. "I haven't had good Thai in months."

Bennett smiled. "We'll need to go into the city."

Cris clapped his hands over his mouth in mock horror. "Oh no. You're making me leave Brooklyn?"

"Can you do that?" Bennett did his best to look serious, but he was too busy trying not to laugh. "It's okay, you know. I go to and from the city and I survive."

"I think you're gonna regret it. You can take the boy outta Brooklyn, but you can't—"

"Yeah, yeah, I get it. Come on, Brooklyn boy, I'll make sure you don't offend the locals."

Cris started to follow him but stopped. "Wait!"

Bennett turned with a mixture of curiosity and a touch of frustration. "Yes?"

"Let me dump my bag behind the bar. I can pick it up tomorrow." Cris vanished into Cowboys and Angels and dumped the bag in the locker room. He noticed Dan's raised eyebrow as he emerged. "I'm going out with Bennett. I don't want to lose my costumes."

"Okay. See you in the morning."

Dan turned back to his customer, and Cris made his way through the crowd again to reach the door. He sighed with relief when he was finally back on the sidewalk.

"All done?" Bennett asked.

Cris nodded. "Done. This Thai food better be worth me leaving Brooklyn."

"Dude, it's worth leaving the whole damn state for."

"Lead on—"

"Please don't say Macduff."

Cris grinned at Bennett. "Would I do that?" He laughed out loud as Bennett rolled his eyes. "Come on. You have to, don't you? Everyone says that."

He made his case all the way down the street until Bennett shoved him and told him to shut the fuck up. Then Bennett had to apologize to a family passing by, and Cris laughed until tears ran down his face.

IF ANYTHING, the Thai hole-in-the-wall was even more jammed with people than Cowboys and Angels had been, but the minute Bennett was spotted by an elderly waiter, they somehow found a tiny table for two squeezed in the far corner.

Cris waited until they'd settled before he pounced on Bennett. "They know you here?"

"I come here most weeks. I love Thai food next to my mama's cooking."

"That's cute, in a Hallmark romance kind of way."

Bennett shook his head. "You're not a blonde girl, and I'm definitely not a prince." Cris eyed him for a long while, and Bennett went a little pink. "What?"

"You're a prince to me," Cris said eventually.

"That's even more sickly sweet than the Hallmark comment."

Cris started laughing. "Yeah, I guess it was."

Bennett grinned, and they both snickered again.

After a while Cris looked around. "Are they gonna bring menus?"

"Uh… no. They usually just bring me what I like. I guess they'll just bring more of it."

"Huh. What if I'm allergic to something you like?"

"Are you?" Bennett demanded.

"No," Cris said reluctantly.

"Well then."

Cris thought Bennett sounded far too smug. "I hope the food arrives soon. I'm ready to eat the table." The rumble of his stomach was loud enough to reach Bennett.

"You can wait."

But someone must have heard Cris, because suddenly the table was full of fragrant spicy food.

Cris groaned as more and more little plates filled the table. "This looks amazing. Is this all for us?"

Bennett heaped his plate with noodles and rice. "Yep. Eat up, because it tastes even better."

Cris would have replied but his mouth was full of spicy garlic chicken and vegetables. He figured Bennett would be eating the same food, so he didn't have to worry about garlic breath.

They didn't speak as they ate. Instead they rushed to fill their stomachs and chased the last of the food in the bowls. They washed the food down with chilled Thai beer.

Finally Bennett sat back, his hands on his stomach. "You like?"

"I more than like." Cris moaned in appreciation. "I think this was the best food I've ever eaten."

"I came here soon after I moved into the apartment, and I've never stayed away. I'd eat here every night if I could."

"Thank you for bringing me here." Cris looked around and saw an eclectic mix of locals and tourists laughing and eating, enjoying the food and the ambience.

Bennett pinked. "You're the only person I've ever brought here."

"I am?" That thought warmed Cris.

"It was kind of my place. I didn't want anyone else interfering."

"So why did you invite me?"

"I don't know." Bennett bit his lip.

"You don't?" Cris didn't want to embarrass him, but he wanted to know.

Bennett sighed. "I like you, Cris."

"Like me?" Cris teased.

"Oh, fuck off," Bennett said easily enough. "I like you a lot, okay?"

"I like you too." Cris grinned at him. "You're so cute."

Bennett growled at him. "I'm gonna live to regret ever telling you this."

"Yes, I think you are."

"I wanted to share this place with someone special."

Cris leaned over the table and brushed Bennett's hand. He wanted to kiss him, but he knew Bennett wouldn't be ready for any public display of affection yet. Then again, they were touching hands. "Thank you for sharing it with me."

Bennett looked at their joined hands. "You're welcome. Will you come back to my place?"

"Now?" At Bennett's nod, Cris said, "Yes." He didn't have to think about it.

"I'll get the check."

They argued briefly about who was going to pay. Cris was all for going dutch, but Bennett pointed out he was the one who'd invited Cris, and he was going to pay. Cris huffed and left a tip that was almost as much as the check. Bennett told him he was stupid, but Cris ignored him. Then Bennett waved goodbye to the elderly waiter, and they left, Bennett's hand in the small of Cris's back. So much for worrying about public affection. Maybe Cris should have taken that kiss.

Cris snorted when Bennett opened a door next to the restaurant. "You didn't tell me you lived upstairs."

"I said I lived close by." Bennett led the way up the stairs to the fifth floor. "I learned to love Thai."

"I bet you did."

Then Bennett opened his front door. One minute Cris was standing in the hallway, and the next he was in Bennett's apartment, up against the wall, and Bennett's mouth on his. Cris let out a garbled whine and sank into the kiss.

Bennett ran his tongue over Cris's lips. "You taste so good—ginger and garlic."

"It's a good thing you like both."

"I love the taste of spicy Cris."

"Kiss me again."

Bennett cupped his ass and hauled him closer. He ground his mouth on Cris's, and they rubbed frantically, their hard erections pressing into each other.

"Uh... Benny?"

The last voice Cris wanted to hear interrupted his haze of arousal, and Bennett tried to yank away from his embrace.

CHAPTER 9

BENNETT TRIED to pull away from Cris again, but when it became clear Cris wasn't going to let him move, he gave Cris a scowl and turned to stare at his brother. "Mikey? What's wrong? What's happened?"

It didn't take a rocket scientist to realize Mikey was in a bad way. He looked whiter than newly laid snow and had dark marks under his eyes. His mouth trembled, and he wrapped his arms around himself as though that were the only thing keeping him together.

"I'm… sorry for interrupting you," he said. There was a note of betrayal in his expression, and Cris winced as he realized what Mikey must be feeling. If he were in Mikey's shoes, he'd feel betrayed too. Cris had rejected him and then gone after his brother.

Bennett looked between Cris and his brother, clearly torn about what to do. "I—"

"It's okay." Cris finally let Bennett go and gently shoved him toward his brother.

"What's happened, Mikey? I thought you were gonna be at Mama's." Bennett looked at him and then went to Mikey, wrapped his arm around his shoulders, and led him into the living room.

Mikey collapsed onto the sofa as though someone had cut the strings to his legs. "I was. I had an argument with her again. She won't let it go."

Let what go? Cris followed them into the living room but stayed by the door and leaned against the doorframe. He didn't want to interfere.

Bennett tugged Mikey closer. "The wedding?"

"Why does she have to push it all the fucking time?" Mikey clutched at his hair. It was damp and stuck up in spikes. "I love Mama, but she won't give me a break."

"Don't curse," Bennett said automatically. "She just doesn't understand why you're stalling. You've been engaged for a long time. She just wants to see you happy and settled. You know what she's like."

Mikey groaned and hid his face in his hands. "She's not the only one. Julianne keeps asking me when we're gonna set a date too."

"That's... not surprising," Bennett said. "They've been talking a lot recently, making plans."

"Why can't they leave it alone?" Mikey let out a noise that seemed a cross between a sob and a shout.

Cris sighed, and both brothers looked over. He wanted to walk over and shake some sense into them, but he knew it would just cause more trouble. "I think I should leave you two to talk."

Bennett looked troubled, but he nodded. "Can you get back okay?"

"I think I can manage the subway."

"I'll call you tomorrow," Bennett said.

"Sure." Cris gave him a brief smile and looked at his brother. "Take care of yourself, Mikey."

Mikey managed a short nod, and Bennett mouthed, "I'll call you."

With nothing left to say, Cris left the living room. He'd opened the front door when Bennett said, "Cris, wait."

Cris turned, only to be manhandled against the wall. He opened his mouth, but Bennett was there and thrust his tongue down Cris's throat. Finally Bennett raised his head, his lips glistening and his eyes unfocused. Cris licked his lips. His voice was unsteady. "I thought we'd done this already."

"I know, but I didn't want you to think...." Bennett scrubbed his hand through his hair. "I don't want you to go, but...."

"I know, I know." The anger drained out of Cris, and he cupped Bennett's jaw. The short hairs tickled his palm. "It's okay. Go back to Mikey. Call me tomorrow. No, wait. I'm working all day now."

"I'll come into Cowboys and Angels. I've got a meeting with my father in the morning about one of our projects, but after that I'm free."

"Okay." Cris brushed Bennett's lips and gently pushed him back. "Go on. Go be big brother."

Bennett nodded, but he waited in the doorway for Cris to reach the stairs before he closed the door. Cris jammed on his hat as soon as he reached the sidewalk and shivered in the cold night air. He stood for a moment, unsure of his next move. The cold was too much, and he contemplated finding a gay bar to dance his frustration away... and maybe something more. But even as the thought entered his head, he pushed it away. He had an early start at the bar the next day, and much as he'd like to dance and hook up with someone, he couldn't push away Bennett's face. Bennett was easing his way into Cris's life, and he should walk—no, run—before he got his heart broken.

"Too fucking late, Peters," he muttered.

An elderly woman holding a tiny Chihuahua cast him a suspicious glower, and Cris quit talking to himself and headed for the subway.

The train was crowded, so he stood, squashed between a black man a good six inches taller than him wearing a spicy cologne and a stocky white guy immersed in a soccer game on his phone and oblivious to Cris and everyone else. For the first time, Cris felt really short. How the hell did even shorter people feel everyday as others loomed over them? He gave a sympathetic look to a tiny woman pressed up against the door by a large backpack, and she scowled at him. Cris sighed and went back to squinting at the stocky guy's phone. He didn't mind soccer when there was nothing else to watch.

BY THE time he reached home, Cris was tired and grumpy. Aside from the meal, nothing had gone right that day. His mood wasn't improved by a conciliatory message from Marlon on his voicemail—if telling Cris to get his butt into the club the following night could be called conciliatory. Cris deleted the message. He wasn't in the mood to deal with his ex-manager. As he had his phone in his hand, he did remember to set an alarm and then a second one just in case. Mornings weren't his thing.

Cowboys and Angels wasn't a long-term replacement job, but it would help for now. And Dan had a point—other clubs had been trying to headhunt him for a couple of years. Maybe he'd see if any of them were still interested in an old man. Marlon could take a hike. Cris couldn't help a vicious grin at the thought of Marlon trying to run the show with just the newbies.

The apartment was freezing, but Cris didn't bother to turn on the space heater. Instead he warmed up by having a quick shower and changed into flannel pajama pants and a faded band T-shirt. He cleaned his teeth, collapsed into bed, and snapped off the light, but now he was wide-awake and restless. After a night in the club, he was usually very tired. Now he just felt frustrated.

"Dammit," Cris muttered as he rolled over onto his stomach and grabbed a pillow to hug close to him. He closed his eyes and tried to relax enough to sleep, but his brain wouldn't stop whirring, mainly with the thought of Bennett, his face flushed with arousal. He'd looked beautiful. Cris could have watched him for an eternity.

Just like at the studio, he wanted Bennett, and Bennett definitely wanted him. Bennett's cock had been as hard as nails pushed up against his. If they'd stayed like that for much longer, one or both would have come in their pants just like before. His dick thickened at the thought of Bennett rubbing against him as he had, thinking of nothing but their pleasure for once, the usual worry on his face erased by arousal. Cris wanted that, but he wanted more too. He wanted everything with Bennett—fucking, sucking, whatever the man was prepared to offer him. But what would that be? A relationship in the closet? Hiding from his parents? Cris clenched his fists and dug his nails into his palms, but it didn't stop him wanting Bennett.

Almost unwillingly he rolled onto his back, pushed down his pajama bottoms, wrapped his hand around his cock, and jacked it slowly. Then he stopped, flung out a hand, and fumbled for the lube on the nightstand. He flipped the top, squeezed some onto his hand, and coated his shaft. Then he slid his thumb over the head of his dick and dipped briefly into the pear-shaped slit. Hissing at the pleasure, he squeezed his cock, jacked it long and slow, squeezed again, tried to imagine it was Bennett's hand giving him pleasure as he had at the studio, compared Bennett's roughened skin to his own.

"Fuck," Cris exhaled slowly. He closed his eyes again and sank into the fantasy of Bennett straddling his hips, Bennett's hand around his cock, telling him to hold on to the headboard while Bennett brought him to orgasm. He grabbed the headboard with his right hand, planted his feet firmly on the bed, and jacked off faster until he was almost… not quite… fucking there. Cris yelled into the darkness as he climaxed and ropes of come spurted over his stomach.

For a moment he lay in the mess of the bed, in sticky and sated contemplation, still not quite ready to let go of his fantasy. In his mind Bennett jacked over him until his come mixed with Cris's. Then he collapsed beside Cris, breathless and chest heaving as he recovered his breath. The darkness seemed heavier, the room redolent of their come and sweat, their pants and gasps and....

Cris sighed. Perhaps he ought to take up writing romance novels. He sat up and found the tissues to mop himself up. Then he balled them up, aimed them in the vague direction of the trash can, pulled up his pajama bottoms, and settled back down to sleep. The buzz he'd felt before was muted, and though it took him a while, sleep finally took him away.

THE DAMNED alarm was an unwelcome intrusion in his dreams. He turned it off and rolled over onto his front, burrowed under the blankets, and drifted back to sleep. He cursed and growled at the second alarm, but he forced himself to sit up.

When he made sure both alarms were turned off and not left on snooze, he saw someone had left him a message. Expecting it to be Marlon, he tapped the screen.

See you later.

He smiled at Bennett's brief message. Whatever was going on in his head, Bennett wanted Cris, and Cris would remind Bennett of that if things got tough. As he stared at the screen another message appeared.

Get up!

Cris growled but he was chuckling too. Bennett had remembered his comment about mornings.

It was Saturday, and Cowboys and Angels was teeming with regulars and a surprising number of tourists. Cris didn't have time to think as he served drinks and put up with Ariel's endless teasing about his amateur skills as he poured beer, and helped Dan with deliveries. There was an issue with one of the pumps, and some of the regulars got a little restless at missing out on their favorite beer, but Dan told Cris to stay behind the bar while he went down to the cellar. One thing Cris was good at was dealing with a restless crowd, and he got them trying other beers and coming back for more.

Gideon was sitting at the bar, going through what looked like invoices. At one point he glanced at Cris. "You've got good people skills."

"I take my clothes off for a living in front of hordes of drunken women. I have excellent people skills." Cris grimaced as he remembered his current employment situation. "At least, I did have."

Gideon didn't look surprised. "Dan told me what happened."

"I'm still not sure if he fired me or I walked out. Either way, I'm out of a job."

"Do you want to go back?"

"Hold on." Cris's attention was distracted by a customer. Then it got busy again, and Cris didn't have time to resume the conversation until nearly an hour later, by which time Gideon had vanished upstairs.

Someone else appeared, though, and Cris was even more pleased to see him.

"Hello, stranger. I was beginning to think you'd forgotten me," he said as Bennett leaned on the bar. He wanted to lean over and give him a kiss, but he knew this wasn't the time or the place. "Do you want a drink?"

Bennett grinned at him. "Yes, but no."

"Which is it?" Cris asked.

"I've got to go home and work for a couple of hours. If I start drinking now, I might not stop. Give me a soda instead?"

Cris nodded and poured a Coca-Cola into a tall glass. Bennett smiled at him and handed him a five-dollar bill.

When Cris gave him his change, Bennett said, "I'm sorry. My meeting went on for longer than I expected. We've got a project downtown, and it's over budget and overdue. The client's not happy, and Tata's furious. He needed someone to shout at."

"Is it your project?"

"No."

Cris frowned as he processed that. "So why is he shouting at you?"

"Because then, by the time he gets to shout at the people causing the trouble, he's all calm and razor sharp. I'm used to it."

"It doesn't seem fair."

Bennett shrugged. "It's family."

"I guess so," Cris said doubtfully.

"It's our family," Bennett amended. "Tata needs someone to off-load to. I'm that person."

"Who do you shout at?"

"I used to shout at Mikey, and he'd shout at me, but he's not really coping at the moment."

That was the understatement of the year, and it left Bennett handling not only his brother's meltdown but his father's anger too, with no one to listen to him.

"You can off-load at me. I don't mind." Cris's offer was impulsive, but it was genuine, and worth it, judging by Bennett's smile.

"Thanks. I mean it, thank you. I can't remember the last time I had someone watching my back."

Cris frowned again and opened his mouth to speak, but Dan came over.

"Hi, Bennett. You can take your break, Cris."

"Are you sure?" It was still busy in the bar, and Cris didn't want to leave them short.

"Yeah. You haven't stopped all day. Be back here in an hour."

"Let's go for a walk," Bennett suggested.

"Where?"

"Does it matter?"

"Okay." Cris went into the back to grab his jacket, and by the time he returned, Bennett had drained his soda.

The cool air was cold and bracing after the heat of the bar, but it was welcome. They fell into pace side-by-side, and Cris told Bennett his revelation the previous night after being stuck between two exceptionally tall people on the train.

Bennett let out a rumble of laughter. "You should hear my sister complain about being short. When we used to ride the train together, she always complained about how many men don't use deodorant."

Cris wrinkled his nose. "Gross."

"It is for her," Bennett agreed.

"At least I got to watch a soccer game."

Bennett tilted his head as he looked at Cris. "You're a silver-linings kind of guy."

"I try to be."

"I like that," Bennett murmured. "I'm not. Sometimes I see the dark side too much."

"Do you suffer from depression?"

"I have in the past. Not as badly as my brother and sister. Does that bother you?"

Cris shook his head. "No, but it's good to know. My mom has depression. But she's finally on medication that seems to work."

Bennett pointed to a pizza place. "I'm hungry. You okay if I grab a slice?"

Cris's stomach rumbled, and he suddenly realized he hadn't eaten anything all day. No wonder he felt hungry. "Sure. I'll have one too." They each ordered a slice and ate it as they continued their walk. Cris groaned in satisfaction as the food hit his empty stomach. "I should have ordered two."

"We can get another one before we go back," Bennett said.

"I think I'm gonna have to. This is the only thing I've eaten today."

"You can't work on an empty stomach," Bennett scolded. "You're definitely getting another slice. What time do you finish today? We could go for dinner."

"I finish at eight. Make it a delivery at my place or bring takeout and you're on," Cris said.

Bennett's lips twitched. "Tired?"

"Exhausted. Bartending is hard work."

"Harder than pole dancing?"

"I'm on my feet all day," Cris complained, "and Ariel is a slave driver."

"I'll come over and massage your feet. Are you working tomorrow?"

Cris furrowed his brow, remembering the quick conversation he'd had with Dan about shifts. "I'm free tomorrow. Then working evenings Monday to Thursday."

"Good. We can sleep in tomorrow."

The purr in Bennett's voice made Cris look at him very closely. "You want to stay the night?"

Bennett threw the trash from the slice into a nearby receptacle and then shoved his hands into his pockets. "Only if you want me to."

"I want you to," Cris said, "although you might have to poke me awake to do anything."

Bennett's lips curved into a smile. "I don't think poking you will be an issue."

They grinned at each other and then laughed as Cris's stomach rumbled again.

"Another slice?" Cris suggested.

"Sounds perfect."

As they munched the second helping, Cris said, "I'm gonna have to learn to eat in the morning on weekends. I'm gonna have to learn to be awake. I haven't seen a Saturday morning in years."

"Do you think you'll be bartending long?"

"I hope not."

"You don't like it?" Bennett asked.

"I can't afford to do it. I have to pay rent on the apartment and the studio."

"I'd forgotten the studio."

"It'll be impossible to find somewhere as good as that for the same price."

Cris turned to Bennett and noticed sauce on his chin, so he leaned over and wiped it away with his thumb. Bennett stiffened, and Cris sighed, but Bennett caught his wrist as he took it away.

"I'm trying," he said.

Cris stuck his thumb in his mouth and licked away the sauce. "I know you are. Just keep reminding me of that."

Bennett nodded, and they circled around back toward Cowboys and Angels. Cris knew Bennett was stepping way out of his comfort zone even walking with Cris, but he had to be patient and give him time.

CHAPTER 10

CRIS STARTED, abruptly woken by the thumping on the door. Sleep-dazed, he looked around and realized he'd fallen asleep on his sofa. In front of him on the table was his untouched plate of ramen—a poor excuse for dinner, but it was all he could be bothered to make. He must have fallen asleep as soon as he sat down.

It wasn't the evening Cris had anticipated. Bennett had texted and apologized for canceling at short notice because he'd been called back into work to deal with a crisis. Cris wondered if it was an excuse, but Bennett sounded sincere, and he'd promised to rearrange the next day.

The other text was from Marlon, furious that he hadn't returned to Forbidden Nightz. Cris's response had been short and to the point.

You fired me. I've got another job.

He ignored the stream of texts that followed. It wasn't worth the stress. His time at Forbidden Nightz was over.

The thumping started again before he'd had a chance to get to his feet. Cris frowned as he headed toward his door, not sure who was visiting him at eleven at night. It didn't sound like Bennett's knock. He grinned when he realized he knew Bennett had a particular knock.

The smile faded when he discovered who was at his door. It wasn't Bennett. Cris's heart sank as he encountered the scowling face of the other Petrovski brother, and he had to take a hasty step back to avoid being punched in the face as Mikey raised his fist to thump the door again.

"Hey, careful," he snapped.

Without a greeting Mikey pushed past him and into his living room and turned on his heel to face Cris.

"What the hell are you doing with Benny?"

Cris pressed his lips together. "It's none of your business."

"He's my brother. That makes it my business."

Mikey lurched forward, and Cris was prepared to shove him back, but Mikey managed to recover his balance. The waft of beer made Cris wrinkle his nose. Mikey was liquored up. Dutch courage perhaps?

"Benny's my brother," Mikey repeated and rolled on his heels.

Cris sighed and pointed to the sofa. "Sit down before you break something. I'll make us coffee."

"I don't need coffee." Mikey's tone was petulant.

"Yeah, you do. Sit."

Cris waited until Mikey had slumped into the sofa. Then he went into the kitchen and swiped his phone from the coffee table en route. He filled the machine with ground coffee and water and texted Bennett as it heated.

Mikey's here. Defending your honor.

The response was almost immediate. *Do you want me to come over?*

Cris smiled. His hero. *I'll call if I need rescuing.*

OK. Still at work, but I can come if you need me.

Thanks.

There was no reply to that, so Cris put his phone on the counter and went back to where Mikey drooped sullenly on one corner of the sofa. "Creamer, sugar?"

"Yeah."

Cris rolled his eyes and went back to the coffee. He fixed it like he had for Bennett, returned with the two mugs, and handed one to Mikey. "How do you know where I live?"

"It was in Benny's contacts."

"So you decided to visit me to warn me off your brother?"

Mikey huffed. "He needs someone to look after him."

Yeah, and that's me. Cris seemed to be the only one who didn't expect Bennett to take care of them.

"Why are you really here?" Cris asked gently.

Mikey looked up, and the hurt in his expression was plain to see. "Why him? Why not me?"

And there it was—the root of the matter. Cris scrubbed his hand through his hair as he thought about the words he wanted to say. "You're a good man, Mikey."

Mikey twisted his lips. "But?"

"I prefer older guys." *More experience, no girlfriend.*

"Is that it?" Mikey was no fool, and he wasn't going to let it go.

Cris let out a long sigh. "You're engaged to a woman. Even if I were interested in you, I wouldn't get involved."

Mikey seemed to curl in on himself. "I love Julianne. We've been together since high school."

"If you love her so much, why are you chasing after me, Mikey?" Cris asked, as gently as he could manage.

"I... I'm just looking for a fuck."

"If that's what you really want, why are you here?" Cris knew too many guys who had married women, had the family and the white picket fence, and went hunting for guys to get laid. He wasn't that guy, and he didn't think Mikey was. "You're falling apart, man."

"I'm not falling apart."

"Yeah, you are."

Mikey had that betrayed look again. "You don't know what you're talking about."

"Mikey, you can talk to me."

"Everyone wants me to talk," Mikey said bitterly. "No one wants to listen."

Cris wanted to lean over and slap him upside the head, because what the hell did Mikey think Bennett had been doing all this time? But he bit back the harsh words and instead gently said, "I'll listen."

For a moment he thought his words had worked. He could see the need in Mikey's eyes, but then Mikey snorted and put down his mug.

"You just want to get into my brother's pants."

"And if I do?" Cris challenged.

"You think Benny is less screwed up than me?"

No, Cris didn't think that, but he wasn't going to betray Bennett's trust. He just kept a steady gaze on Mikey.

Mikey placed his mug on the table and stood. "Benny isn't gonna come out any more than I am. He's just convincing himself he can pretend to them." *Them* being their parents, Cris assumed. He nodded and followed Mikey to the door, and Mikey turned to look at him. "Don't screw up, Lionman. He doesn't deserve it."

"I know."

Mikey sighed again. "I think you do. If he was going to find anyone, I'm glad it's you."

"Thanks, Mikey," Cris said.

For a long moment, Mikey stayed where he was, his gaze rooted to the ground. When he raised his head, there was a maturity and resigned acceptance Cris hadn't seen before. "Thanks for being honest. I needed to hear it, even if it was hard to accept." He walked away without waiting for Cris's response.

Cris shut the door behind him, leaned against it, and let out an explosive breath. Damn, he was in way over his head. *He* needed someone to talk to—not Bennett, obviously. Dan, or Gideon at a pinch, would have to be that person whether he liked it or not.

Exhaustion caught up with him, and Cris yawned. His eyes closed, and he was about ready to sink to the floor and fall asleep, but the sound of a text made him open his eyes. He shuffled wearily to the kitchen counter, picked up the phone, and looked at the screen.

Do you need me?

Cris took a moment to tap out his response, his fingers fumbling over the keys. *All okay. He's gone.*

Okay. Night.

Cris wondered if there was a sense of disappointment in the terse reply. It wasn't that he didn't want Bennett there, but just right then he needed sleep. He'd be better company in the morning. He dumped the cold ramen in the trashcan, placed the bowl in the sink, and headed into his bathroom. He could go to bed hungry for one night. Sleep was more important. He cleaned his teeth, shuffled into his bedroom, and crawled under the covers with a moan of relief. He was almost asleep when the next text arrived. Irritated, Cris cranked open one eye and looked at the screen.

Sleep well.

He managed a *You too*, and then he was thankfully, blissfully asleep. If there were any other texts, Cris was oblivious to their arrival.

CRIS'S HEAD was filled with plans for his painting of Bennett. He knew exactly which building he'd use as the backdrop for the painting—a partially constructed building downtown, it was little more than a shell at the moment. Cris had spent a long time scoping out the building as it progressed, hoping inspiration would strike him, and now, thanks to one of the people involved in the building itself, he had his plan.

He'd gotten up early and spent the morning taking photo after photo of the building. In the early days of the series, he encountered hostility and suspicion from the site workmen. Now, as they moved from site to site, he encountered a lot of the same men. They recognized him, joshed with him, and asked when it was their turn to be featured in one of his paintings. He laughed and joked with them, pleased to be developing a sense of camaraderie. It helped when he was taking photos. Some of the men were Cowboys and Angels customers too, and he'd bought more than one of them a drink at the bar in the hope they'd agree to be painted.

Kneeling on the floor of his studio, Cris spread out the photos. He'd managed to capture the early morning sunlight coming around the edge of the building. It loaned the half-constructed building a sharp, almost-fragile quality, but with a promise of the design to come—much like the man he wanted to paint. Bennett had the possibility of so much more than he was at the moment, yet it was his fragility as well as his experience that attracted Cris to him.

Cris was deep in thought, adding rough sketches to the photos when there was a knock at the studio door. For a second he was irritated at being disturbed. When he was in the flow of things, it was hard to focus on anything else. He sighed, got to his feet, and headed for the door, but his irritation swiftly vanished at the sight of Bennett leaning against the wall, dressed in a navy hoodie, tight blue jeans that molded to his long thighs, and wearing a tentative smile on his face, as though he weren't sure of his reception. Cris held out his hand, tugged Bennett into the studio, and slammed the door shut behind him.

"Well hi…."

Anything else Bennett was going to say was muffled by Cris's mouth as he pushed Bennett against the wall and cupped Bennett's face with his hands. Bennett needed a shave, and his bristles prickled Cris's palms, but he didn't mind that. Bennett flailed a moment, but then he settled his hands on Cris's hips and returned his kiss with enthusiasm. Bennett tasted of the fresh morning air, underlaid with coffee and bacon. Cris ran his tongue along Bennett's lips, and Bennett parted his eagerly. One of them groaned—Cris wasn't sure which one—and the sound was swallowed up between them. Cris slid his hand up through Bennett's dark hair. The curls were cool to the touch. Bennett wrapped his arms around Cris's waist and kissed him harder.

When his lungs protested the lack of oxygen, Cris drew back and looked at Bennett, who blinked, his eyes glazed, still lost in the throes of the kiss. Cris waited until Bennett focused on him again.

"Morning." Cris grinned at him, although it was probably more of a smirk.

"Is it still morning?" Bennett said. "That kiss seemed to last forever."

Cris brushed Bennett's lips again. "Is that a problem?"

"Not for me."

Their lower halves were still pressed against each other, and Bennett's arousal pressed against Cris's. Cris loved the fact they were of a similar height. When he rolled his hips, Bennett gasped.

"I want to suck you," Cris murmured into Bennett's ear. He hadn't intended to greet him like that, but once he had Bennett in his arms, he didn't want to let him go.

Bennett gasped again. "Do it."

Cris had the presence of mind to lock the studio door, just in case one of the artists arrived. Then he kissed Bennett hard again, as his hands went to the waistband of Bennett's jeans and he slowly undid the buttons. It was starting to be a habit here. Then he blinked. Bennett wasn't wearing any briefs. Cris's mouth went dry.

"You went commando?"

Color spread along Bennett's cheeks. "I thought… I hoped this would happen at some point. I just thought I'd make things easier."

"Baby, I am not complaining." Cris wrapped his hands around Bennett's hard shaft and smeared his thumb over the tip.

"Baby?" Bennett didn't look impressed, although his hips didn't seem to care what name he was called as they thrust forward and pushed his cock through Cris's hand.

"Sorry, it just slipped out," Cris apologized.

"I can think of a way you can make it up to me," Bennett gasped, "starting with you on your knees in front of me and your mouth wrapped around my dick."

Cris tightened his grip around Bennett. "Is this what you want?"

"Uh-huh." Bennett placed his hands on Cris's shoulders and pushed down insistently.

Cris snickered, but he obediently sank to his knees without letting go of Bennett's cock. He looked up and gloried in Bennett's darkly desperate, needy expression. The tile floor was hard on his knees, but he pushed that aside and licked the tip of Bennett's cock, determined to draw as many moans as he could out of him.

HALF AN hour later, he'd sucked Bennett until his knees gave way, and Bennett returned the favor, only with a much quicker result. Cris had been on a knife-edge to climax from the second Bennett's hot spurts reached his mouth. They cuddled on the floor with Bennett's head on Cris's shoulder as they recovered their breath. When Bennett raised his head, he noticed the laid-out photos, and Cris led Bennett over to inspect them.

Bennett sat down cross-legged and gave a rueful laugh as he tapped one of the photos. "I can't believe you're painting this building."

"Is it one of yours?"

"This is the project that's causing me problems. See this bald spot? This is because of this building."

Cris looked where Bennett pointed, but all he could see were neat brown waves. "You hide it well."

"I'll be lucky if I have any hair left by the time this building is complete."

"What went wrong?"

"The project manager badly miscalculated on materials, and the budget has tripled."

Cris winced. "I bet your dad's not happy."

"He's livid. He fired the project manager yesterday, and he was threatening to fire me until I pointed out I'd had nothing to do with the site. I've been focused elsewhere. In fact this is one of Tata's pet projects, and he took his eye off the ball. That's why he's making such a fuss."

Biting his lip, Cris held back the anger he felt at Petrovski picking on Bennett. He was Bennett's father, and it was family as well as business. "He's feeling guilty?"

"Yeah. And he should be." Bennett didn't hold back. "The profit margin is small enough as it is on this project. It's also thanks to my father doing this for a golfing buddy."

Cris wondered if it was about time Bennett's father took a step back from the business or maybe retired. Again, that wasn't something he could discuss. If he were Bennett's boyfriend, that would be a different matter.

Bennett gave a long sigh and rubbed his temples. "I think he wants to retire, but he doesn't think we're ready to take over the company—we being me or Mikey. And he really wants a Petrovski at the helm of the company."

"What do you want?" Cris asked cautiously.

Bennett picked up one of the photos, the one with the morning sunrise. "I wouldn't have taken my eye off the ball, and Mikey has a better grasp of materials than most of the managers working for us."

"He does?" Cris couldn't keep the surprise out of his voice.

"I've never met anyone better. He wants to be a carpenter because he loves working with his hands, but in his head," Bennett tapped his temple, "he can design anything. He understands materials in a way I never will. I can design a building, but he's the one who'll take my designs and tell me what to build it from."

Cris shook his head. "Why aren't you doing that?"

"Because that's not Tata's vision for us. We're his sons, and we're here to run the company."

"And marry good women and produce little Petrovskis to take over."

"That too," Bennett agreed. His eyes were ranging over the photos, so he didn't see Cris's angry expression. "These are good photos. Tata would love to see these. He'd also like to know how you got such good access to the site. So would I."

Cris smirked at him. "An artist has to keep his secrets." At Bennett's derisive hum, he said, "It's nothing illegal. I don't go onto the site, but I do spend a lot of time by the gates. Look at the angle."

Bennett studied the photos carefully. "These are taken by the gates. But these?" He tapped a section over to the left. There was a note of suspicion in his tone.

"I know the janitors to a lot of buildings. I spend a lot of time on rooftops."

"You'd make a good spy."

"With this hair?" Cris pointed at his orange locks. "You'd see me coming a mile away."

"I prefer seeing you coming up close and personal," Bennett murmured, "but I get your point."

Cris warmed at Bennett's words, but he laughed it off. "I'm not that subtle. Once I decide on a building, if I need better access, I'll talk to the construction company. I've got photos of my paintings for them to see, and a lot of the workmen know me now. They vouch for me." He laughed at Bennett's surprised expression.

"Why do I not know about you?"

Cris shrugged. "I don't know. What do you think? This is the building where I wanted to paint you, but if you'd prefer one you've been involved with...."

It would be hard to redo his plans, but he could find another subject for the building.

"How hard would it be for you to start again?" Bennett asked, more perceptive than Cris had given him credit for.

"I'm in the early stages. Do you have another location in mind?"

Bennett nodded. "I do. Do you have a hard hat and boots?" At Cris's nod, he smiled. "How about I show you?"

CHAPTER 11

CRIS GOT out of Bennett's Toyota, shoved his hands in his pockets, and stared long and hard at the row of partly constructed one-story houses. One of them was almost finished compared to the others.

They weren't what he expected. They'd driven away from the office buildings and into a residential area. The surrounding houses were neat, but they'd seen better days. This wasn't a high-class Petrovski development, and yet there was the Petrovski name on the sign.

Bennett moved, and Cris turned to look at him.

"I don't understand," he said.

"I know this isn't as dramatic as an office building, but you want to paint me, and this…." Bennett waved an arm around. "This is me. Or at least as me as it's going to get for a while."

"You built this place?" Cris asked.

"This is my project, not a Petrovski development, despite the name."

"You're building a house for yourself?"

Bennett's expression was a mixture of pride and self-consciousness. "These aren't for me. I'm involved with a project for veterans. My company is building the houses at reduced cost for a veterans' group. They've got a joint project with a city-sponsored urban renewal program. I wasn't joking when I said Mikey can work out the cost of materials down to an inch. Mikey and I sat and planned out five houses, with potential for further development if this works. The charity has big plans. This is only the first step."

Cris stared at him, at the houses, and at him again. "You designed these?"

"Yes."

"You're incredible, Bennett Petrovski. Do you know that?"

"It's no big deal," Bennett said, although his expression said the exact opposite. "It was Mama who suggested it. They needed help and approached one of her boards. I was looking for something to do, and Mikey was on board as soon as he heard. He's also going to fit out the kitchens when the houses are built. I'm a qualified electrician too. Tata made a fuss because it takes us away from the family business, until Mama asked him to front a fundraiser to build the houses. She can twist him around her little finger."

"I'd like to look inside," Cris said.

"Sure. You'll need the hat."

Cris grabbed his hard hat—he'd learned very quickly he wasn't going anywhere near a site unless he wore a hat, boots, and hi-vis jacket. He also picked up his camera. He couldn't promise Bennett he would use these houses. They didn't really fit into his theme, but he would take the camera in case inspiration struck him.

"This way," Bennett said. He unlocked the gates and led Cris across the site to the house that was most complete. "Careful where you walk."

Cris followed him into the house and looked around. The house was small inside with a living room at the front, dining room and kitchen side-by-side toward the rear, three bedrooms and a bath upstairs. And in the basement, a front room, a back room and a kitchen. So far the house walls had been framed out, floors were down, and the kitchen was partly constructed. Bennett smiled at him, pride beaming from him, and it was like someone had switched on a light.

"I looked at refurbishing old homes. It would have been cheaper. But someone donated the property, and with the city program, it made sense to build new homes."

"It's gonna be great," Cris said, and he meant it. The houses were being built for people who needed them. It wasn't just another prestige office project.

"Gideon put a lot of money into this project too," Bennett said. "He was one of the first people I approached. Thanks to him a lot of other business people put their hands in their pockets."

Cris wasn't surprised. He'd learned that Gideon was the head of a large holdings company in New York. Gideon didn't make a big thing about it, and Dan seemed to largely ignore the fact Gideon was wealthy.

Bennett pulled out a roll of paper and spread it over the kitchen countertop. He noticed Cris's look. "I like working on paper first. Like you with your paintings."

Cris nodded. Although he documented everything on his laptop, all his plans started out in his sketchbook, which was currently in his pocket.

"We wanted the houses to look like the others on the street."

Bennett talked through the plans as they walked through the house, and Cris took out his camera and snapped photos here and there. Nothing struck him, but sometimes inspiration took a while. Then they looked around the rest of the site, but the other houses were barely more than the outer shell. Bennett's chatter faded as they reached the last house.

"This isn't doing it for you, is it?" he said.

Cris smiled at him apologetically. "Not so far, but it's not a quick process. Sometimes it takes weeks before I have an idea in mind."

"You can stick with your original plan if you want."

"I'd like to come back at different times of the day. A lot of my paintings are set at sunrise." Cris shrugged. "I was always up when the sun rose."

Bennett nodded. "I'll drive you back out here one morning." He moved, and just then the sun shone through the unglazed holes in the house where the windows should be.

There was an *aha* in Cris's mind. "Stay exactly where you are," he ordered.

Bennett was startled, but he stayed still while Cris shot off a score of photos. They were quick—nothing more than a place marker—but he wanted to capture the light on Bennett's face. It was always about the way light framed the men in his paintings. It made them vibrant and larger than life. Then he quickly sketched Bennett while he waited patiently.

Finally Cris looked up and grinned at Bennett. "All done. You can move now."

"'Bout time," Bennett grumbled, but his smile gave him away. He rolled his shoulders. "Are you ready to go home?" At Cris's nod, he asked, "Do you want something to eat?"

"Yeah, if it involves steak." Cris had promised himself a steak dinner to cope with the week ahead.

"We'll go back to my place. I've got steak and all the fixin's in the fridge."

Cris raised an eyebrow. "Enough for two?"

"I was gonna invite you to dinner to make up for the last time you were there and we were cock-blocked by my brother."

"Where is he today?" Cris wasn't in the mood to have a repeat performance of that or the previous night.

"He's at Julianne's."

Cris grunted and Bennett looked over. "Just leave it."

It was more of a plea than an order, and Cris gave a curt nod. He didn't want to spoil the mood. They'd had a good day together.

"Have you got beer?"

Bennett furrowed his brow. "Uh, no. I think Mikey had the last bottle."

"Let's swing by Cowboys and Angels. I need to confirm what time Dan wants me to start. He told me one time, Ariel another."

"Done."

Cris waited for Bennett to lock up the site and then slid into the car beside him. "Thanks for taking me here."

Bennett turned to look at him. "I've never done that before."

"I'm honored."

Bennett patted Cris's thigh. "You're welcome."

AT COWBOYS and Angels, Bennett took care of the beer while Cris looked at the staff roster. He was penciled in at the end. Cris took a photo of his shifts and went in search of Bennett, who was nowhere to be seen.

"Where's Bennett?" he asked Dan.

"Your boyfriend's talking to Gideon," Dan informed him.

They still hadn't officially had the "we are boyfriends" talk since the night he was fired, but after the last few days, Cris decided it didn't need to be discussed. Bennett was his boyfriend even if it did make his heart leap every time it was mentioned.

"Lionman." Gideon's boom echoed across the bar.

Cris restrained an eye roll, caught Dan's smirk, and turned to see Gideon and Bennett walking toward him. "Gideon."

Gideon's smirk was even larger. The bastard knew how much it wound him up. It wasn't that he was ashamed of being Lionman, but Cris liked to separate his personal and professional lives. He also knew it would be fatal to say anything out loud. He'd never hear the end of it.

Bennett reached him first, and his smile soothed Cris's ruffled feathers. "Sorry I disappeared. Gideon wanted an update on the housing project."

"It's about time I came out to have a look," Gideon said.

"You'd be welcome any time," Bennett said.

Cris nodded. "You're doing a good thing."

To his surprise, Gideon looked… Cris tried to recognize his expression… embarrassed.

"It was Dan's suggestion. We have veterans as customers, and Dan tries to keep an eye on them. We've lost a few from PTSD over the years." Silence fell between them for a moment, until Gideon sighed and said, "When Dan heard about Bennett's project, he thought it was a way to do something practical."

"Without you we'd never have funded the project," Bennett said. "You convinced my father it was a good public relations exercise."

Gideon beamed at him. "Business strategy is something I'm good at. So is Dan, by the way, although he needs more practice." He smiled tenderly at Dan, who was out of earshot at the other end of the bar. Dan looked up, and his smile back at Gideon was so intimate Cris would have been embarrassed to witness it if he hadn't seen that exchange all the damn time.

"Did you get the beer?" Cris asked Bennett.

"Not yet."

"What do you want?" Gideon asked.

Ten minutes later they were en route to Bennett's apartment and, hopefully, steak and baked potatoes. Cris's mouth watered at the thought.

"What time do you have to be at work tomorrow?" Bennett asked.

"Not 'til five. I'm gonna do my laundry and stuff before I go in."

"Would you like to stay the night? I've got an early start, but I could drop you home before I drive to the site."

Surprised at the offer, Cris looked over at Bennett, whose attention was fixed on a Lexus reversing onto the street. "I'd like that. Are you sure?"

"Yeah." Bennett's voice was husky. "I'm sure."

He didn't glance over, but Cris could sense his smile, and Cris smiled too.

THE LAST time Cris had been at Bennett's apartment, he'd been distracted and looking around hadn't been at the front of his agenda. Now he looked around curiously. It was a large, spacious apartment, probably four times the size of Cris's. It suited Bennett and was decorated in browns and creams—neutral tones, but comfortable—and a polished wooden floor. Cris eyed the large overstuffed leather sofas with envy. He'd kill for just one of them, although each sofa was almost larger than his apartment. One wall was stacked to the ceiling with shelves filled with vinyl. If they ever lived together, they'd be classified as hoarders.

"Nice place," Cris said.

Bennett looked around as though he were seeing it for the first time. "I like it. I've lived here since I left college. It was my grandma's place, and I spent a lot of time here as a kid. When she died, she left it to me in her will."

"You own the place?"

Bennett flushed. "The Petrovski company owns the building."

Cris nearly whistled out loud. His parents were comfortably off, but this was a different league. Besides, any help from Cris's parents stopped abruptly when he refused to become an engineer.

"It suits you," he said.

Bennett eyed him suspiciously, but he seemed to relax when he saw Cris's expression. "I'd hate to have to move. Mind you, if I did, Mikey would be in here like a shot. He loves the place as much as I do. Ready to eat?" Cris's stomach growled in response. Bennett laughed. "I guess that's a yes, then."

Cris followed Bennett into a small kitchen.

Bennett pointed to a stool by the breakfast bar. "Take a seat. The potatoes are already baked. I've got to heat them up.

"You prepared them earlier?"

Color spread along Bennett's cheeks. "I was going to ask you to dinner."

Cris felt a warm feeling spread through him. Whatever was going through Bennett's head, it was obvious he wanted to spend time with Cris. "If you feed me with steak, I'll always say yes."

Bennett handed him a bottle of beer. It was from a microbrewery Cris hadn't heard of, but Cowboys and Angels had a reputation as the place to go to for good beer. Dan was always researching new breweries, especially local companies. They'd held a couple of beer festivals, organized by Ariel and much appreciated by the regulars.

He took a chug—not that he was a connoisseur, Cris was just as happy with cheap beer from the tap, but it seemed to have an orange flavor.

Bennett eyed him perceptively. "Do you like it?"

"It's different." Cris took another swallow. "Stronger than I'm used to. Don't tell me you brewed it."

Bennett laughed. "No, but I really like it. I try all the new beer. You don't have to drink it if you don't want to." He laughed as Cris clasped his bottle to his breast. "There's cheap and nasty beer too."

"Thanks," Cris said flatly, but then he grinned.

Despite Cris's protests, Bennett swapped out Cris's beer and kept the orange beer for himself. The conversation was light and easy as Bennett worked around the kitchen. Cris offered to help once and was told to sit and stay. Bennett admitted he didn't like eating on the sofa—a hangover from his grandmother's rules—so they would eat at the breakfast bar. The delicious aroma of baked potatoes and frying onions filled the air, and by the time Bennett presented him with a loaded plate, Cris was ready to eat the furniture.

Cris chased around the last piece of steak on the plate and sighed in contentment before he chewed. "That was epic," he declared and belched contentedly.

Bennett was maybe a mouthful behind, but he too sighed and burped in agreement. Then he sat back and rubbed his belly. "I needed that."

Cris belched again. "I don't think I'll ever need to eat again."

He was going to have to be careful. He couldn't afford to eat like that if he was going back on the stage. But today he would enjoy himself.

"Let's go in the other room," Bennett said. "I've got ice cream for later."

Cris followed Bennett into the main room, collapsed contentedly on a sofa, and closed his eyes for a moment. Bennett picked out an album, and the room filled with Stevie Nicks's haunting vocals.

"Is this okay for you?" Bennett asked.

"More than okay."

Cris opened his eyes as the sofa dipped and found Bennett staring at him intently. He sat with one leg tucked under him, and his eyes were huge, dark, and framed with thick lashes.

"You have very pale skin," Bennett murmured.

"Pasty skin and freckles," Cris agreed.

"Beautiful skin." Bennett traced one finger over his cheekbone. "You must burn in the sun."

"All the time. That's why I work at night. I'm a vampire."

"But you don't go poof at sunrise."

"Not usually."

Cris turned to face him and mirrored his pose. Bennett took Cris's hand and laced their fingers together. Cris waited. He had a feeling Bennett had something on his mind, and finally Bennett brushed his lips over Cris's knuckles.

"Tell me," Cris ordered.

"What?"

"Tell me what's on your mind."

Bennett exhaled a long breath. "Mikey called me this morning. He told me about his visit to you last night."

"What did he say?"

"That he felt I betrayed him. I knew he liked you, and it wasn't fair for me to be in a relationship with you."

Cris frowned. "I've made it clear I'm not into him, and I *am* into you." He emphasized the word so there could be no mistake, and Bennett tightened his fingers around his.

"I'm into you too, in case that's not clear."

"But?" Cris was sure there was a *but* coming.

Bennett sighed again. "I'm not out."

Cris waited.

"You're the first man I've ever been open about."

"Thank you." Cris placed a kiss in the palm of Bennett's hand.

"But my parents don't know." Bennett gasped.

"Don't you think they'll find out?"

"Mikey's threatened to tell Tata."

Cris was ready to find Mikey and strangle him for being a selfish stupid brat. "Do you think he will?"

"Not if he doesn't want his own secret out," Bennett said grimly.

Stalemate.

"Bennett, I'm not in the closet, and I have no intention of going back in." Cris had to get that out there, because he'd been open with the world for a long time, and he intended to stay that way.

"I know. And I *will* tell my parents, but on my terms, not with Mikey threatening me."

"He's just hurt and lashing out."

"I know." Bennett looked into Cris's eyes. "I just need you… I'm asking you… to be patient with me."

Cris didn't answer immediately, and Bennett's expression grew bleaker, but finally Cris nodded. "You can set the pace of our relationship."

Bennett sat back, relief written in his expression.

"As long as you understand that while you associate with me, people will think you're gay," Cris warned.

"They can think what they like. If I don't start making out with you, it's all rumor."

"Denial, denial, denial."

"It's worked for centuries," Bennett said.

But at what cost? Cris gently tugged his hand away and sat back. He felt as though he'd gotten on a bus that was out of control and there was no Keanu Reeves to save the day.

CHAPTER 12

"NICE VIEW."

Initially Cris didn't realize the compliment was aimed at him because his head was down and his ass up as he hunted for a coin that had slipped out of his hand and rolled under the bar. He found the missing coin with a crow of triumph. Then he looked up and remembered just in time to move away so he didn't bump his head against the solid wood of the bar. Bennett leaned over it and grinned down at him.

Cris grinned back. "Hey, I didn't expect to see you tonight."

He stood and almost leaned over to kiss Bennett. He pulled back just before it became obvious and covered himself by dropping the coin in the till.

"Mikey wanted to come, and I knew you were working tonight." Bennett didn't indicate that he'd seen Cris's aborted move.

They hadn't seen each other since the previous Monday morning when Bennett dropped him home on his way to work. Bennett had been working long hours on a crazy project, and Cris hadn't called either because he welcomed the space. He needed some time to think after the night at Bennett's. They'd slept wrapped around each other but, aside from lazy early morning hand jobs, they hadn't pursued anything further. There was a tension between them that Cris had to admit mainly came from him. His conversation with Bennett had unsettled him. He'd thought—hoped—they were progressing into something more. And discussing it with Dan hadn't helped either. Cris got the feeling Dan believed the Petrovskis were a lost cause.

"It's good to see you." Cris looked around to see Dan and Bradley serving the other customers. "What do you want to drink?"

Bennett pointed to an IPA and leaned against the bar as Cris poured the beer. "You're getting better at that."

Cris grimaced as he thought about how much beer he'd wasted initially. "I'm getting a lot more practice."

"Still no luck getting your job back at the club?"

He placed the beer in front of Bennett and took his money. "I'm not even trying. I haven't called Marlon, and he's ignoring me now. I don't wanna go back there. Thankfully Dan's offered me as many shifts as I want. One of their new guys quit after the first shift. He couldn't deal with Ariel."

Bennett frowned. "What about the studio? I thought you were getting ready for an exhibition."

Cris forced a smile. "I was, but I've postponed it. I'm not gonna be ready in time. Another guy at the studio is taking my place."

"You can go next time, right?"

"If there is a next time."

"I'm so sorry, Cris," Bennett said gently.

"Yeah, me too." From the sympathetic look on Bennett's face, he didn't need to say how upset he was at losing the exhibition. Months of hard work and long hours planning, and all that preparation had gone to waste. It would be years before he got another chance like that, if it happened at all. The gallery had been a big deal. He took a deep breath and plastered a smile on his face. "It's okay. I'd have struggled to be ready in time anyway. I still haven't started your painting."

"There'll be a next time," Bennett rumbled. "And you'll be ready then."

Cris couldn't help but smile. "You sound very sure."

"I have faith in you. I've seen your work, remember?"

If Cris hadn't been working and in Cowboys and Angels, he'd have dragged Bennett off to a quiet corner and kissed him until the man was breathless. It had been so long since someone had shown unconditional support in him.

"Thank you. I appreciate it." He let his eyes do the talking for him.

Bennett smiled, but Cris got distracted by another customer, and Bennett vanished into the evening crowd. Cris didn't have time to do more than occasionally seek him through the mob. If it had been the other way around, he would have been easy to spot. Not many people had flame-colored hair, but Bennett blended in with everyone else.

And didn't that just sum up their current situation?

Cris was pouring a beer when he heard a shout from across the room. He looked over to see Mikey about to throw a punch at one of his friends. He was nose-to-nose with another guy, fists already clenched.

"Don't you dare call me a fucking faggot!"

Mikey's words resonated in the sudden silence in the bar.

The other man, at least thirty pounds heavier than Mikey, sneered at him, and Mikey snapped, jumped on him, and shoved him to the ground. He laid punches into him faster than Cris could keep track of.

"Oh fuck," Dan swore and charged around the bar. From the other corner of the room, Gideon and Bennett rushed toward the brawling pair. Gideon pulled Mikey off the prostrate man and pushed him to one side, and Bennett wrapped his arms around his brother, but Mikey shook him off, and Bennett staggered backward. Cris managed to steady him before he fell. Bennett muttered his thanks and pulled free to confront his brother, but Dan was there first, hands on his hips and his expression furious.

"What the hell is going on?" He reached down to pull the man on the floor to his feet. His nose bled profusely, and his left eye was red and would probably swell shut. Dan handed him a tissue.

Mikey gasped for breath, his face red from exertion and anger. He stabbed a finger at the other guy, and his knuckles were red and swollen. "He called me a faggot." He spat the words out angrily.

Dan spun on the other man who took a step back in the face of Dan's anger. "What the hell, Trey?"

"It was a joke, Dan," Trey said hastily. "Just a joke about the song he was singing."

Dan didn't look as though he found it funny. "I'm a fucking faggot, Trey. Do you want to say that to my face?"

Despite the fact he was much larger than Dan, Trey cowered away. "No. No. I'm sorry."

"Do you want to press charges against Mikey?" Gideon asked him. "I can call the cops right now."

"What?" Mikey spluttered.

If anything, Trey looked more shocked than Mikey. "No, no, we're good. Aren't we, Mikey?"

Mikey, who had looked like he wanted to tear Trey limb from limb until the possibility of charges against him were mentioned, nodded furiously. "We're good."

"So you don't want to press hate-crime charges against Trey?" Dan asked, steely-eyed.

"What?" Trey protested.

"What? No! It was a stupid heat-of-the-moment thing," Mikey protested. "Tell him, Trey."

"I'll never say fag—that word—again," Trey assured them.

Dan took a deep breath. "Gideon, take Trey away and clean him up. And while you're doing that, explain what's gonna happen if I do hear him use that word again in my bar."

Gideon smiled viciously at Trey, who went even paler, and Cris couldn't help but feel sorry for him.

Then Dan turned on Mikey as Gideon and Trey walked away. "This is your last fucking warning, Mikey. Go home and get your shit together. If you cause trouble again in Cowboys and Angels, you ain't coming back. Do you understand?" Mikey nodded, but Dan said, "That's not good enough. Say it out loud."

"I understand," Mikey muttered.

Dan's expression softened a fraction, and he ruffled Mikey's hair. "You're a mess, kid. Get your shit together before you get it kicked in."

Mikey huffed loudly and looked around as though seeking support. It didn't escape Cris's notice that no one stepped forward until Bennett grabbed Mikey by the arm and said, "I'm taking you home. Get your coat."

"I don't wanna go home," Mikey said.

"Tough," Bennett snapped. "I think everyone's had enough of you tonight."

Dan patted Mikey on the back. "Your brother is right. Go home and get some sleep."

Mikey scowled, but he shrugged on his jacket and cap. Bennett looked over at Cris and mouthed an apology, and Cris smiled at him. He was disappointed their evening had ended so abruptly, but he understood family came first.

The brothers disappeared out the door, and Cris returned to his post behind the bar. He poured beer after beer and chatted to customers about anything except Mikey Petrovski. At some point Gideon emerged with Trey, who was sporting an impressively swollen eye and a penitent expression. Dan handed Trey a beer, and Trey vanished back to his friends.

Gideon sighed as he sat down opposite Cris. "Gimme a Coke please. I swear that boy's got nothing between his ears except cotton candy."

Cris snorted and handed Gideon the soda. "Trey or Mikey?"

"Either... both," Gideon sipped his drink. "That's better. I had to do a lot of talking to get Trey to understand. It was a throwaway remark to him. He had no idea Mikey was going to react like that."

"He's not the sharpest tool in the shed," Cris agreed.

Gideon looked around. "Where's Mikey?"

"Bennett took him home before he could get into more trouble."

"Good call. Is Bennett coming back?"

"Not as far as I know. He's gonna have his hands full with Mikey."

"Fair enough. Could you give Dan a hand to clean up after closing? Bradley has to leave early, and I've promised Trey I'll run him home. He took quite a pounding from Mikey."

The last thing Cris felt like doing was staying up another few hours to clean the bar, but the money was useful, and he wasn't working the next day. He'd promised himself a few hours at the studio, but he could do that later in the day. "Sure. Do you need me in tomorrow?"

Gideon shook his head. "No, it's fine. You've worked hard this week."

"It's probably the hardest work I've done since my dad made me work on a ranch on vacations in high school. Cured me of wanting to be a cowboy."

Gideon chuckled. "Are you sure you don't want to come work for me for good? You're the best temp I've ever had, and I could give you a hat and spurs if you want to be a cowboy."

"No need, Gideon. I've already got a hat and spurs just waiting in my closet." Cris winked at him.

"Whose bar is it?" Dan asked as he walked past with a tray of dirty glasses.

"It's your bar, darlin'."

Dan rolled his eyes, and Cris grinned because it was an ongoing battle. Gideon couldn't quite let go of the reins.

"I like doing a good job. I don't care if it's stripping or bartending," Cris said.

Gideon eyed him thoughtfully. "You're wasted as a stripper. Have you ever thought of management?"

Cris laughed out loud. "What would I manage?"

"We'll see," Gideon said cryptically. He didn't pursue it any further, and then they got distracted by a crash from the kitchen.

Cris got to his feet. "I'll deal with it. You're front of house. I can sweep up a few glasses."

"As I said, maybe you need to extend your repertoire."

"There's not much call for stripping dishwashers." Cris chuckled and headed into the kitchen to find Bradley surrounded by broken glass.

"Stay there," Cris said. "I'll sweep you a path to get out."

"Thanks, man," Bradley said gratefully. "I can't wait for this evening to be over."

"You're not the only one," Cris agreed as he backed out of the kitchen to get the broom from the janitor's closet.

THE LAST thing Cris expected to see was Bennett dozing against his front door when he finally made it back to his apartment.

He hunkered down beside him. "Hey."

Bennett opened his eyes and blinked sleepily as he tried to focus. "Hey."

"You must be frozen." Cris stood and tugged Bennett to his feet. When Bennett staggered, Cris held him up until Bennett regained his balance. "I didn't expect to see you here. Where's Mikey?"

"He's with Julianne." Bennett yawned and hopefully missed Cris's eye roll.

Cris decided not to say anything. What could he say that hadn't been said before? He fished out his keys, opened the front door, and pushed Bennett ahead of him.

Bennett groaned and said, "It's so warm in here."

"How long were you waiting?" Cris threw his keys in the pot and took off his coat.

"What time is it now?" Bennett looked around for a clock.

"About six."

"Not long. Maybe an hour."

"Why didn't you call?"

Bennett didn't respond beyond a mumble, but Cris suspected Bennett was asleep on his feet. He gave up on the questions, guided Bennett over to his bed, and pushed him down onto the covers. With some hindrance from Bennett, he stripped off his coat and outerwear, and pulled off his boots. Then he pushed and pulled until Bennett was under the comforter. He was asleep before Cris had finished and in the middle of the bed. Unless he moved Bennett, there was no room for Cris, and he didn't have the heart to disturb him.

Oh well.

Cris grabbed spare pillows and a comforter out of his closet and dumped them on the sofa. It wasn't the first time he'd had to sleep on the sofa, and it was reasonably comfortable. He puttered around, changed into his pajamas, and cleaned his teeth. Then he switched off the lights, felt his way to the sofa, and lay down. It took him a while to get to sleep. His brain was whirring and acutely conscious of the man sleeping not ten feet from him. Cris hugged a pillow to him, wishing it was Bennett. A snuffle and snort from the bedroom made him grin, and he relaxed enough to sleep and finally sink down into grateful darkness.

CRIS WOKE to the aroma of coffee and a hushed but heated discussion. He lay for a few minutes trying to work out why he wasn't in his bed and who was in his apartment.

"I don't care. You were drunk again. Dan is right, you've got to get your act together."

Cris blinked and stared up at the ceiling. Bennett was in his apartment, and he was obviously talking to his brother. Cris wondered if he should make it known that he was awake, but he didn't want to get involved with their argument.

"Trey called you a faggot. So what? He didn't know you were gay. Trey calls everyone a faggot. You know that." Another long pause, and Cris really wanted to use the bathroom and hopefully drink coffee. But Bennett hadn't finished. "You can't go on like this. You're engaged to a wonderful woman. Mama and Tata are waiting for you to set the date."

Nothing changes. They were both still padlocked and bolted in the closet. Cris gave up waiting and sat up, but Bennett had his back to the sofa and didn't notice him. He padded into the bathroom to do his business, clean his teeth, and splash water on his face. By the time he came out of the bathroom, Bennett had finished his call and was glaring into a mug of coffee.

"Morning." Cris focused on pouring the dark brew into his favorite mug. He reached into the fridge for creamer and then doctored his coffee until it was the right consistency and color.

"Morning," Bennett almost growled. "I'm sorry for waking you."

"What time is it?"

"Eleven."

Cris grunted and took a sip of coffee. Five hours sleep—no wonder he was tired. "Thanks for the coffee."

Bennett looked almost surprised, as though he'd forgotten he'd made the pot. "Right. You're welcome."

He smiled at Cris, who ignored him and got up to raise the blinds. The rain beat steadily down. The world outside was as miserable and gray as Cris felt.

"Is everything all right, Cris?" Bennett sounded uncertain.

"Yeah."

"Well… I guess I'd better go home."

Cris flopped down on the sofa and kicked the covers to one side. "Good idea." He closed his eyes and ignored Bennett. He'd just woken up and hadn't had nearly enough caffeine to deal with Bennett's issues.

Obviously disconcerted by Cris's unfriendly tone, Bennett said, "Okay."

Cris waited. He heard Bennett shuffle around to get his things, and then he heard the front door open, and a quick gust of cold air made him shiver. He stayed where he was on the sofa. It was too fucking early to face the world.

CHAPTER 13

THE FRONT door closed, and Cris breathed a sigh of relief, but he didn't bother to open his eyes. He knew he'd been an asshole, but how many times did he have to hear Bennett push his brother and Julianne into a life of misery? It was starting to screw with Cris's mind. He couldn't go on like this without talking to Bennett. What Mikey decided to do was his business, but Cris didn't have to watch it unfold.

He'd always had an issue with men who used women to cover their homosexuality. He also knew men and women had been forced into unwanted marriages for centuries, and they'd had no choice in the matter. But he'd seen the other side. He'd had an aunt who discovered her husband was gay. She found a strange man in her bed when she returned a couple of hours early from a day out with her children, and things unraveled at lightning speed. She'd been left to bring up five kids while her ex-husband jumped into the gay scene with both feet and not a backward glance at his distraught family. It left Cris with a sour taste in his mouth because he knew most of his issues stemmed from a deep dislike of his uncle.

The man was a dick—he'd been a dick in his marriage and a dick in the divorce. Not every gay guy deserted his wife and kids. Cris knew that. He sighed and draped an arm over his eyes to block out the light. Perhaps Mikey would be different. He'd loved Julianne for a long time. If he got his act together, he'd be a good man.

The sofa dipped. Cris jumped, he'd been so lost in his thoughts, he hadn't heard a sound. He opened his eyes to discover Bennett scowling at him.

"What the hell's wrong with you this morning?" Bennett demanded.

"You were going."

"I changed my mind. Answer my question. What the hell's wrong?"

"I could ask you the same." Cris snapped back and then cursed silently. It was hard to miss the scowl was tinged with worry. Bennett was scared. Scared Cris would cause trouble? Scared Cris would leave him?

"I don't know what you mean."

"I know," Cris sighed. "That's what makes it so fucking sad."

Bennett wrinkled his brow. "Cris, you're talking in riddles."

"I heard you telling Mikey to set a date for his wedding."

"Oh."

"Yeah. Oh." Cris could do the flat tone too.

"You don't approve."

Cris shook his head. "It's none of my business."

Bennett gave a derisive snort. "I'm making it your business."

Okay. If Bennett wanted it that way. Cris sat up and let rip with both barrels. "Mikey is gay. *G.A.Y.* Why the fuck are you forcing him into a marriage he doesn't want?"

"You don't understand."

"Make me understand."

Bennett huffed, but finally he said, "It's not me or my parents forcing Mikey into this. They don't know about him, obviously, but he's the one who wants to get married. He's been talking about it for years."

"Mikey wants to get married?" Cris blinked in confusion.

Bennett nodded. "Yeah. This is his idea."

Now Cris didn't know what to think. "But you're the one telling him to get married."

"Only because Mikey insists it's going to happen. He's like a rollercoaster. Up and down. Up and down."

Cris knuckled his eyes. "I haven't had enough coffee for this conversation."

"I hear you," Bennett said grimly.

"I'll make another pot."

The conversation died as Cris clambered to his feet and set about making more coffee. Cris was glad for something to do with his hands, and Bennett stared at the wall of DVDs as though he'd never seen them before.

Cris placed two mugs on the table and sat down again at the other end of the sofa from Bennett. He picked up one of the mugs, took a long swallow, and focused his attention on Bennett. "Why would Mikey want to marry a woman?"

"He says now he's bisexual."

"Yeah, and there's nothing wrong with being bi, but there's a lot wrong with planning your wedding at the same time you're planning to screw around with guys."

"He likes women."

"Or he wants to like women?" Cris had known a ton of guys who identified as bi. Some loved women and men with equal enjoyment— Gideon was very open about his bisexuality—but some guys admitted they used bisexual on the way to gay. Cris didn't have an issue with that if they didn't screw up other people on the way. He sighed. His ex-uncle had really done a number on his psyche.

"I don't know," Bennett said helplessly. "I don't care if he's bi or gay, but he either goes through with this wedding or he does the decent thing and breaks it off with Julianne before it goes too far."

"Are you pushing him to fix a date to force the issue?"

"I thought it would work. He ignored me when I told him to break it off, so I thought pushing him might change his mind. All it's done is make him angrier and more confused. Julianne is upset, and my parents keep asking when they're going to set a date."

Cris drank his coffee as he processed the new information. It explained a lot, but none of it helped. Mikey was still hell-bent on charging down the wrong path, and Bennett was tying himself up in knots.

"Fuck, this is a mess," Bennett sighed.

"A total shit fest," Cris agreed.

He got up and fixed two more coffees. When he came back to the sofa, he sat closer to Bennett, put an arm around his shoulders, and gathered him close. Bennett folded in on himself and rested his head against Cris's chest. He was warm and solid in Cris's arms, and Cris pressed a barely there kiss into Bennett's hair.

"I'm sorry I've dragged you into it." Bennett's voice was muffled as he talked into Cris's T-shirt.

"Mikey started it by trying to jump me in the john at Cowboys and Angels."

"I gave him hell about that," Bennett said.

"It wasn't his finest moment."

"I hate the fact that it affects us too."

Cris held him tighter. "It doesn't have to."

Bennett sat up, and Cris reluctantly let him go.

"Until I tell my parents, I'm still stealth dating you. I'm a man over thirty. I'm not a good role model to Mikey if I'm sneaking around with my boyfriend."

Cris chuckled. "I've heard of blind dating and speed dating, but stealth dating is a new one."

Bennett glowered at him. "You know what I mean."

"Yeah, I do. And to be honest, I don't think we've been that stealthy. It's not like most of the bar doesn't know we're involved."

"I've been waiting for word to get back to Tata."

"Then maybe you should consider telling them first?" Cris suggested gently.

Bennett nodded and scrubbed a hand through his usually neat hair. It stuck up everywhere. "Just give me a little time?"

Cris swallowed back his urge to ask how much time and instead combed through Bennett's slightly greasy locks with his fingers. "You need a shower."

"I need to get to work." Bennett looked at the time. "Dammit, I'm gonna catch hell from Tata for being late."

He picked up the mug and gulped down the contents, his throat working hard. When he finished, he leaned over to kiss Cris hard on the mouth, and then he was gone, leaving behind his sweet coffee taste on Cris's lips and the feeling that nothing had been resolved.

Cris sighed, finished his own coffee, and wondered what to do next. For a moment he was tempted to shove a DVD in the machine and waste the afternoon watching TV. But it was lunchtime, and he really needed to do his laundry. He packed his sports bag with his dirty clothes and impulsively grabbed his sketchpad and pencils.

Once his clothes were in the machine and Cris had settled himself in his favorite seat, he took out his sketchpad and stared at the blank page. He wanted to draw the long curve of Bennett's jaw, the sweep of his neck and the crest of his Adam's apple—strength and grace, masculinity and vulnerability. He could see it on the page, even though he hadn't made a mark. The noises and bustle around Cris faded away as he started to sketch with quick lines and no detail, just the silhouette of Bennett's jaw and neck.

One sketch became two and three, all focused on Bennett's body—the strength of his shoulders, the delicate wing of his collarbone. He couldn't stop until everything that was inside him was there on paper.

"You're very good."

The comment distracted him from his work, and he looked up to find a bright-eyed, elderly gentleman with a shock of white hair smiling at him. "Uh... thank you."

"You're doing it all from memory."

"Yes."

"Someone you know?"

"Yes." Cris dialed back the impatience, but he was anxious to get back to his sketching.

"You must love him very much."

Cris stared at the man. "I... what makes you say that?"

The older man reached into his jacket pocket and drew out a battered leather wallet, flipped it open, pulled out a faded photograph of two men, and handed it to Cris. From the clothes they were wearing Cris hazarded a guess that it was taken in the sixties.

"This is you?" Cris asked.

"I'm on the left. Philip is—was—my partner. He died last year. If I had any talent, I could still draw every inch of him from memory."

"I'm sorry for your loss," Cris said automatically. "How long were you together?"

"Sixty-five years. We met at college."

"That's a long time."

"A lifetime." The man blinked rapidly, pulled out a worn handkerchief, and blew his nose noisily.

"Did you ever get married?"

The man nodded. "Just before he died, just because we could. I didn't really care, but it mattered to Pip, and if it mattered to him, it mattered to me." He held out his gnarled hand for the photo. The artist in Cris noticed the young man's hand in the photo compared to the old man's hand, misshapen by arthritis and covered in liver spots.

A lifetime of living between the two hands. "Anyway, thank you for listening to an old man's tales."

Cris handed over the photo, and the man tucked it away. "Thank you for sharing them with me."

The old man went to get up and leaned heavily on his cane. "I'm sorry I disturbed you."

"Wait, sir." Cris touched his arm. "Are you in a rush?"

"No, I'm still waiting for the machine." He pointed to a machine almost at the opposite end of the row.

Cris hurried on. "I'd like to draw the two of you. A gift. A thank-you for sharing your story. It would just be a quick sketch."

"I wasn't asking for...."

"I know. But I'd like to. May I know your name?"

"Charles," the man said as he sat down again. "Charles, not Chas or Charlie."

"Charles," Cris repeated. "I'm Cris, not Christopher." He'd made it plain how he wanted to spell his name from an early age.

"And your man?"

"He's not yet. But he might be. His name's Bennett."

"That's... an unusual name."

Cris caught the hesitation and looked up, but the man was smiling at him. "I guess so. The photo?"

Charles handed it over again and sat quietly while Cris took a few moments to plan the sketch and then focused on his work. He worked with fierce concentration and brought the two young men to life. When he was done, he handed it to Charles.

The old man stared at it for a long while, and the paper trembled as his hand shook. Cris waited patiently by his side until Charles looked up. "Pip could be by my side again." His voice was hoarse from unshed tears.

"Thank you." Cris pulled out an envelope from his bag and slipped the sheet of paper into it. "This should protect it until you get home."

"You've done this before," Charles said.

"Once or twice. For the right people."

Charles carefully stowed the envelope in his inside jacket pocket and got to his feet. He held out his hand and shook Cris's. "Once I met Pip, there was never anyone else."

"You were very lucky to meet him."

Charles nodded. "Indeed I was, Cris. You take care now. And tell Bennett how you feel about him before it's too late."

He walked slowly away before Cris could reply. Cris sighed. Bennett made his knees tremble and his dick grow hard just at the thought of him. But love? It was too soon to be talking about love, wasn't it?

"BENNETT! BENNETT! Bennett!"

The crowd chanted and roared as Bennett stripped off his leather pants to reveal a black satin jockstrap and then shimmied around to bend over and show his perfect, plump buttcheeks. The shrieks of appreciation grew louder because damn, that was a fine ass.

Jostled by the screaming women, Cris waved his fifty-dollar bill, desperate to tuck it in the jockstrap of the god on the stage. "Bennett! Bennett! Come here!"

Bennett swayed around the front of the stage, accepting all the adulation and the bills. Cris waved again, and then the god stood over him. Cris smiled up at him and showed his adoration in his expression. He tried to add his money to the collection, but Bennett stepped back, his expression disgusted.

"Not you. I don't want you touching me. Take him away."

Devastated, Cris dropped the fifty dollars on the ground, and the bill was immediately stepped on, vanished under the sea of high heels. Hands clamped around his biceps, and he was dragged back by two burly security guards. His last sight was of Bennett writhing in front of a woman.

Cris opened his eyes, covered in a cold sweat and his heart pounding. He shivered despite being under the comforter. Fuck. That was a dream he didn't want again. Where the hell had that come from? He sat up, scratched his armpit, and grimaced as the waft of stale sweat hit him.

"You stink, Peters. Shower, shit, and shave."

His phone beeped, and he squinted at the screen.

Can you do shift tonight? Start 8?

Cris sent a quick affirmative to Dan. The money was useful, and until something better came along, he couldn't afford to turn down shifts.

But he needed coffee first and to wash away the stench of sweat. Then he could work up another sweat at the gym, spend the afternoon on his latest painting before his shift at Cowboys and Angels, and try to put Bennett Petrovski out of his mind for a while. His conversation with the elderly man had left him unsettled. He didn't want to fall in love with Bennett only to be rejected. It wasn't love at first sight. Lust, yes. Not love.

Cris shuffled toward his coffee maker, filled it with fresh grounds because he'd forgotten to set it before he went to bed and shuffled into the bathroom. Half an hour later, with two large mugs of java inside him and showered and shaved, Cris felt able to face the world with bared teeth. Heaven help any asshole in the gym who hogged his machine. Cris was ready to tear them a new one.

As he laced up his boots, his phone beeped again. Cris growled, praying Dan didn't want him to come in earlier. He needed some studio time, for his headspace as much his art.

Can u do shift 2nite?

Marlon, not Dan. Cris couldn't believe Marlon was still trying his luck. Cris hadn't been back to Forbidden Nightz since he walked out—or was fired, depending on where the gossip came from. Nor had he been responding to Marlon's texts. Why did Marlon still think Cris would jump when Marlon snapped his fingers?

"The Lionman is dead. Long live Cris."

That wasn't as upsetting as he thought it would be. Maybe it was cutting off his nose to spite his face, or maybe it was time to move on, from the Lionman as well as the club. He texted one word back to Marlon and switched off his phone before Marlon could respond.

No.

Cris picked up his gym bag. Now for a little Cris time.

Chapter 14

By the time Cris reached Cowboys and Angels for the evening shift, he felt more in tune with the world. Snow had started to fall. Cris loved snow, and it soothed his soul. Crunching through the first layers left him red-cheeked and happy.

He'd had a good day—a hard workout at the gym and a gentle at-a-distance flirtation with one of the personal trainers who was really too young for him, but his wide-eyed admiration was good for Cris's ego. Then he spent the afternoon lost in his latest painting of a spotter working at the docks. Cris had caught the concentration on his face as he worked, and he was satisfied with the way the painting was going. It didn't strictly fit in with the construction series, but he could always change it to "men at work." He hadn't thought any more about Bennett's painting. He needed photos of the housing development first, and he'd have to get out there before it progressed much further.

Cris's good spirits lasted as long as it took to push the door open and find Mikey at the bar. That was not the Petrovski he wanted to see. Cris groaned and hoped Mikey would behave tonight. He wasn't in the mood to handle another meltdown. It was unfair, but he still struggled to understand Mikey's desire to marry when it was clearly not what he wanted. Mikey was involved in an animated discussion with two other guys and didn't notice he'd come in. He looked happy enough, but there was no sign of Bennett.

Dan waved at him from behind the bar, and a couple of regulars nodded their welcome. Cris headed into the back and divested himself of his coat, gloves, and hat and took a deep breath. If Mikey decided to cause more trouble, Cris would drag him out and tell him some home truths, starting with his aunt's story.

On cue, Dan pushed open the door and grinned at him. "Thanks for covering Bradley's shift. The dude can barely sit up."

"You're welcome." Cris bit his lip. "Dan, if Mikey—"

Dan shook his head. "He's under strict instructions to keep his shit together this evening or he's banned for life."

"Will he listen?"

"If he doesn't, he's out the door. Gideon was right. He's a fucking time bomb. I dealt with Ariel, and I'm not letting Mikey take her place." Dan gave Cris a quick one-armed hug. "We'll be fine. Now get out there. We've got happy hour soon." Dan gently pushed Cris to the door.

"Yes, boss." Cris hoped Dan's confidence was justified.

They stepped out into the barroom, and Cris nodded a hello to Luis, who was working the far end of the bar, and smiled at a young guy holding out a bill. Cris served him and then the elderly man behind him.

Mikey waited for Cris's attention. He grinned sheepishly. "I'm sorry about the other night, man. Trashed, ya know?"

Cris gave him a curt nod. "Sure. Excuse me." He turned to the next man, a thirtysomething Hispanic guy with huge twinkly eyes. "What can I get you?"

"Five Boroughs Hoppy Lager, thanks." The guy narrowed his eyes. "I know you." Cris waited for the usual comment about keeping his clothes on, but the man snapped his fingers. "You're Mr. Eight."

"That's right. You were there?"

"Yeah, I was Mr. Fifteen. I remember your hair." He turned to Mikey. "You were there too."

Mikey shook his head vehemently. "You've got the wrong man. Sorry. It wasn't me." He backed away as quickly as he could, panic in his eyes.

Mr. Fifteen frowned as he looked after him. "Strange. I don't normally forget a face, especially one as gorgeous as him."

"Ya barking up the wrong tree there, man." The man next to him gave a rumbling belly laugh. Of course it had to be Trey. "Mikey's not a faggot. No offense, Cris."

Cris gave him a thin smile. "None taken."

Mr. Fifteen opened his mouth to argue, but Cris caught his eye and gave a quick shake of his head. Mr. Fifteen waited until the other guy left and then said, "It is the same guy?"

"Yeah. Here's your beer," Cris placed the glass in front of him.

"I didn't realize he's in the closet."

Cris sighed as he saw Mikey's panicked look from the other side of the room. "He's doing the hokey-pokey at the moment."

"Oh, one of those. What a shame. He's a luscious piece of chicken."

The man was virtually drooling.

"You can forget that idea," Cris said sharply. "He's not your prey."

Mr. Fifteen held his hands up in surrender. "I'm sorry. Is he yours?"

Cris's scowl deepened at the implication. "He's a friend, and I'm looking out for him."

"Okay, okay. Hands off. I get it. Oh, never mind, this one is way more my type."

Cris had turned away to serve another customer, but he registered the purr from Mr. Fifteen. "What?"

Mr. Fifteen gave a nod to the man coming in the door, covered in a layer of snow. Oh, deep fucking joy. There was no way Cris was letting Mr. Fifteen anywhere near that man.

Cris snorted. "Good luck trying your hand with that one."

"Not one of us?" He looked disappointed.

"He's mine." Cris smiled viciously.

The man held his hands up. "I get it. He's yours. Hands off."

"Just make sure you do."

Cris moved away, not wanting to continue the conversation. Then Bennett looked around, saw Cris, and smiled tentatively, and Cris smiled in return. It was going to be a long night before they could talk.

"So you have history," Mr. Fifteen said. "Looks like I'm out of luck tonight."

"Maybe you'd do better down at Pinkies."

Mr. Fifteen shrugged. "I like it here. The beer's better. I'll find someone to talk to."

He wandered away, and Dan joined him. "Wasn't that Mr. Fifteen?"

"Yup, and he can't take his eyes off the Petrovskis. I warned him off."

Now it was Dan's turn to snort. "He'd have more luck with Chuck."

Chuck was a fiftysomething longtime customer and a veteran. Bigger than Gideon, he hated queers and regularly talked about how he'd dealt with them when he was in the Marines. He "put up" with Dan because he liked the beer. Dan was sure the man was another closet case, but he didn't cause any trouble beyond boasts of past action when he was liquored up. Since Dan and Gideon became a couple, Chuck kept his mouth shut most of the time.

"This dude is half Chuck's size," Cris protested. "You be mopping him off the floor if Chuck got hold of him."

"Chuck is a pussycat."

Cris shook his head. "Pussycat is the last thing I'd call him."

"You just don't know him as well as I do."

"I'd like to keep it that way. I've got one highly strung male on my hands already."

Dan smirked. "You have that. Changing the subject, I think we'll be shutting early this evening. There's a nor'easter that's turning into a blizzard and they're going to close mass transit. Gideon's keeping an eye on it, and if it looks bad, we'll probably close about midnight."

"Okay, I'm not going to complain about that."

Cris gave him a brief smile and then went back to serving. He caught Gideon making his way over to Bennett, but he deliberately didn't pay much attention to their conversation. He didn't have time to focus because there was a sudden influx of snow-covered guys. Dan, Cris, and Luis did their best to deal with all the customers, but there was a brief jostle for service at the bar. Gideon yelled at them, and they settled down to wait their turn.

The rush died down after a couple of hours, and it was Cris's turn for a brief break. Cris hurried into the office and took the opportunity to close his eyes. Sometimes he sat at the end of the bar and drank soda while he chatted to whoever was around, but this time he didn't want any chance of being collared by Mr. Fifteen for more information on Mikey. The man hadn't taken his eyes off Mikey the entire evening.

"Hey."

Cris opened his eyes at the greeting to see Bennett kneeling beside him. "You shouldn't be in here."

"Dan said I could. I wanted to talk to you."

"Talk?" Cris waggled his eyebrows because he wanted to do more than talk. "How about kiss now and talk later?"

Bennett rolled his eyes, but he didn't look averse to the idea. "I'm sorry I've been so busy this week. I wanted to take you out to the project, but Tata's been working me from dawn to dusk."

Cris cupped Bennett's jaw. "It's okay. Don't take this the wrong way, but I needed a little space."

Bennett looked rueful. "I get it."

"It's not that I don't want to see you."

"I nearly called you, just to have someone to talk to," Bennett admitted. "I had an argument with my parents yesterday. They were trying to get Mikey to set a date for the wedding. He got upset and stormed out, and Mama got upset. They wanted me to talk to Mikey, to make him see sense. Then Julianne called me in tears, and the situation got worse. I don't know what to do."

"Mikey is a heartbeat away from doing something really stupid," Cris said. "Don't you get that?"

Bennett's expression darkened. "I'm not stupid. I know exactly what's going through my brother's head."

"I know. It's not my business," Cris said wearily. "You can talk to me anytime, but I'm only going to tell you the same thing."

"Enough about me and my family. What do you need?"

Cris was taken aback by the question. The idea that someone was interested in him enough to care what he wanted caught him off guard. Being part of a relationship, even a secret one, was still new and strange. "I don't need anything."

"Everyone needs something, Cris." Bennett stayed where he was, and Cris was tempted to spill about the nightmare. But a nightmare was nothing like a brother losing his shit and a father who expected him to be the perfect son.

"Wake up, Lionman, your break is over." Gideon's booming voice interrupted them as he burst through the door from the bar and frowned as he took in the situation. "What the hell are you doing in here?" he snapped at Bennett, who flinched away.

"I just wanted to talk to Cris."

"I told you to stay away from him."

Cris blinked. Gideon had? Why?

"In fact I told you if you came anywhere near him, I would throw you out of my bar. And yet here you are worrying Cris."

"Uh, Gideon—" Cris started. What the heck was Gideon talking about?

"This is none of your business," Bennett interrupted. "This is between me and Cris. Stay out of it, Gideon."

Cris groaned. At this rate, he was the one who was going to be thrown out of the bar without a job. No one spoke to Gideon like that except perhaps Ariel. Gideon and Bennett ignored him.

Gideon's face darkened. "Who the hell do you think you are?"

"I'm the one who loves him." Bennett stabbed a finger at Cris, who stared at him openmouthed.

"You what?" Cris said faintly.

A broad smile spread over Gideon's face. "That's more like it."

Bennett seemed to realize what he'd just said. "Oh shit."

The door to the bar opened again, and Dan stepped in. "Where's my barman?"

Gideon laid an arm around Dan's shoulders. "Well, darlin', it seems Bennett here has fallen in love with Lionman and wanted to tell him that he loves him. Isn't that right?"

Bennett nodded faintly and looked ready to pass out. Cris was ready to join him. What had just happened? One minute they were just talking, and the next Bennett was declaring his love for Cris to Gideon. And what the hell was Gideon doing poking his nose into their relationship?

Dan scowled at all of them. "Cris is supposed to be working, in case all of you have forgotten. Bennett, you've had your talk. Now get on the other side of the bar. Gideon, you were supposed to be fetching Cris."

"I tried," Gideon protested, "but they were having a serious discussion."

Cris threw his hands up. "Dan, Bennett said you let him in here. Bennett, you can't just drop this on me and expect me not to freak out. Gideon, what the hell did you think you were doing shouting at Bennett? He's mine. You don't get to shout at him. I'm going back to work if I still have a job, and I expect everybody to leave me alone."

He stomped past them all and back into the bar and zeroed in on the first person who looked as though they wanted a drink. He didn't care who they were, he was going to serve them. He heard some heated words behind him from Dan, but he didn't feel remotely sorry that Dan was reaming out Gideon for interfering in Cris and Bennett's relationship.

They shuffled back into the bar about five minutes later. Bennett nodded at Cris, but he stayed away, and Cris kept his head down and worked solidly for the next hour. Despite the worsening weather conditions, the bar got busier and busier. Gideon made it known the bar was going to close at midnight and told all the complainers they could fuck off. Bennett stayed by Mikey, who behaved all evening. It seemed to have finally connected with him that he was on his last warning.

To Cris's surprise, he saw Mikey talking animatedly to Mr. Fifteen. He seemed to have gotten over his panic at being seen with a gay man. Cris couldn't hear what they were talking about, but there was a crowd around them, and they were all laughing at something Mr. Fifteen said. Even Bennett had a smile on his face. For a moment Cris was jealous. He wanted to be the one putting a smile on Bennett's face, instead of the worry that habitually resided there.

"They seem to be getting on all right."

Cris hadn't noticed Dan by his side. "I don't really remember Mr. Fifteen at the speed-dating evening. He remembers me."

Dan gave him a wry smile. "They all remember you."

"What?"

"All the guys remember you, dumbass. You stand out in a crowd. Nearly everyone is asking about you. And you may not have noticed, but more gay men come here now that you're working here."

Cris was nonplussed. He hadn't really attracted that much attention during the speed-dating event, and nobody had shown any interest in going home with him. He decided to focus on one part of what Dan had said. "How do the regulars feel about the new arrivals?"

Dan shrugged. "The new guys are just like the rest of the guys here. There's been a few comments, but most have taken it okay. They just want to drink and play pool." He narrowed his eyes as he looked at Mr. Fifteen. "I know him from somewhere other than the speed dating, but I'm not sure where."

"He's a cop," Luis supplied as he walked past with a tray of dirty glasses. "He's down at the local precinct."

Dan snapped his fingers. "Of course. I must have seen him when I got beaten up."

"He's interested in Mikey." Cris looked over to the Petrovskis, only to see Bennett staring at him. But he looked away immediately and pretended to focus on the conversation around him.

"God, this is so painful to watch," Dan said. "You two need to get your act together."

"It's not me," Cris protested. "I'm a happy gay man, remember? He's got to decide what he wants. He can't say he loves me and then run back into the closet and slam the door. I don't live like that."

Dan looked at him for a minute and then said, "You're right. I'm sorry. I know they've been giving you a hard time."

"Not hard enough," Cris quipped, but it sounded bitter even to him.

"Maybe you need to remind him who's the boss?"

There was a brief flurry of customers, and Cris waited until they had gone before he answered. "If it were up to me, I'd be showing him who's the boss right now."

"Dude, TMI!" Luis squealed as he walked past.

Dan rolled his eyes. "I've heard you say much worse to your girlfriend."

"I don't know what you're talking about," Luis said.

"I'm your big man, your big man who's gonna fill you up," Cris cooed.

Luis went crimson as Dan laughed at Cris's impression.

Gideon came over and sat on one of the barstools near Dan. "I thought I told you guys to work, not discuss your sex lives."

"Believe me, darling, I haven't even started yet." Dan batted his eyelashes at Gideon, and Cris groaned.

"If you're going to do that, I'm going to work with Luis. I'll just take his phone away from him."

From his end of the bar, Luis raised an eyebrow. "Try it and die."

"You're all fired," Gideon declared cheerfully.

Cris gasped and clutched his chest. "Not twice in one week."

"It's getting to be a habit," Gideon said.

Dan coughed in the back of his throat. "Whose bar is it?"

"Your bar, darlin'."

"Uh… guys?" Mikey waved a glass. "Can I get a top up before you throw us out?"

"Sure, what do you want?" Dan asked.

Cris felt awkward about moving away, but he didn't look at Mikey. He did notice Mr. Fifteen staring over at them, and he nodded at him to let him know everything was fine. Of course he did the two-step with Bennett as they both pretended not to look at each other.

There was a rush to the bar when Dan announced last call. Cris was busy serving drinks and didn't have time to focus on Bennett. Then he bussed the tables and stacked the glasses on the bar, and he laughed and joked with the guys as he took their empty glasses and ignored their grumbles as they whined about the bar closing early. To some of them, the idea of being trapped inside the bar was a good thing. Cris had a feeling Cowboys and Angels meant a lot more to some of the customers than a place to get a drink.

Once Dan called time, and Gideon pointedly opened the door, they shrugged on coats and hats and scarves and shivered as they went out into the snowy world. Cris spent time stacking the dishwasher with the glasses. When he came back into the main area, the only person left was Bennett, who stood awkwardly by the bar.

Cris went straight up to him. "Why are you still here?"

Bennett pushed his hands into his pockets. "I couldn't go home after what I said. Are you okay? You seemed annoyed."

"I was more annoyed at the peanut gallery. I'm tired now. It's been a long day. Can we just go home?" Bennett's eyes opened wide, and Cris realized what he'd said. "I mean, I need to finish up here and go home."

"I'll give you a hand," Bennett said.

Cris realized he wasn't going to get away easily so he handed the tray to Bennett, and they went around the bar and collected the last of the glasses. Bennett helped him wash up while the others cleaned the bar. There was little conversation between the two of them beyond "please" and "thank you," but it didn't feel uncomfortable.

After a short while, Gideon entered the kitchen. "It's time you boys made a move. The snow's getting worse. You'll be stuck here if you don't leave now. Luis's already gone. Dan and I can finish up."

Cris looked through the window to see that the intensity of the snow had increased. "Thanks. Much as I love you guys, I'd rather be stuck at home than here."

"We feel just the same way," Dan assured him as he came in with more glasses.

Cris threw him the cloth and flipped him off. Then he smiled tentatively at Bennett. "Time to go."

"It's gonna be a long walk home. I could go back to Mikey's." Bennett lived near his parents. It would take him at least a couple of hours if the trains stopped running.

"Come back to my place."

The suggestion was impulsive. He was tired, but he could do with Bennett's company. He wanted Bennett to shelter from the snowstorm with him.

Bennett looked at him uncertainly. "Are you sure?"

"I'm sure. Nothing's gonna be running in the morning. Come back to me, and we'll wait it out." Cris smiled and held out his hand. "I've got hot chocolate with cream and marshmallows."

"Is that meant to be a bribe?" Bennett asked in a deadpan tone.

Cris waggled his eyebrows. "Yep. Will it work?"

"Have you got chocolate sprinkles?"

"Uh… no."

Dan snorted. "Get out of here before my man throws you out."

Gideon preened at being called Dan's man. He was so predictable. Dan only had to look at Gideon for the big man to melt.

Cris rolled his eyes. "We're going, we're going. I'll get my coat, and then we're gone."

The drop in temperature hit him as soon as they stepped out of Cowboys and Angels. Cris drew in a breath and wished he hadn't as the cold seared down to his lungs.

Judging from the expression on Bennett's face, he was in pain too. "What's the chance of us getting an Uber?"

"The roads aren't plowed. What do you think?"

"I was afraid you were gonna say that."

"Come on. It won't take more than an hour."

Cris's estimate might have been optimistic. They struggled through the heavy snowfall on the empty streets. Bennett grumbled for a while, but Cris grabbed his hand and told him to quit complaining.

Bennett looked at their joined gloved hands and then at Cris. "You're a 'glass half-full' person, aren't you?"

"I try to be. I want to see the best in life."

"I'm not."

Under the streetlamp Cris watched snowflakes catch in Bennett's eyelashes and stubble. He tugged Bennett close to him. "You've spent so long taking care of Mikey and watching out for your parents, you've forgotten to take care of yourself."

Snowflakes swirled around them, but they ignored the weather. Bennett's whole attention was focused on Cris. "Since I met you I realize you take care of me."

Cris cupped Bennett's cheek, Bennett leaned into the touch, but Cris was sure Bennett didn't realize it. "I like taking care of you." It was true, but it was more than that. Cris had spent his life taking care of people, but it was different with Bennett. He wanted to hold him close and take Bennett away from what made him so unhappy. It was the first time he'd felt so protective about anyone.

"I like it," Bennett admitted.

"Let me take care of you, Bennett."

"Take me home?"

Cris frowned, not sure what Bennett wanted. "You want to go to your home?"

Bennett shivered, and his teeth chattered. "I want to go to *your* home. I'm freezing."

"Let's go. I can warm you." Cris let his gaze heat up.

"I get the feeling you're not talking about hot chocolate and sprinkles," Bennett said unsteadily.

"I can think of other ways of warming you," Cris agreed.

CHAPTER 15

IT TOOK another twenty minutes, but finally they were home. Cris slammed the front door, mentally apologized to his neighbors, and told Bennett to shed his coat, hat, and gloves. Bennett raised an eyebrow, but when Cris just stared at him, he unbuttoned his coat, and Cris cheered inwardly and did the same. The second they were stripped of outerwear, Cris backed Bennett against the wall and pinned him only with his gaze. He cupped Bennett's jaw, and Bennett swallowed hard.

"I've been very patient," Cris purred.

"You have?" Bennett sounded doubtful.

"I have."

Bennett rolled his eyes but rested his hands on Cris's hips. "You'd better get on with it then."

Cris leaned in and scraped his stubble against Bennett's. They both shivered, and when he did it again, the sensation traveled to Cris's cock. He placed his mouth against Bennett's ear. "I'm all about touch."

Bennett shivered again. "Show me."

"You're wearing too many clothes." Cris took a half step back and slid his fingers under Bennett's sweater. He stroked the undershirt over his flat abdomen, and even through the fabric, Bennett's muscles rippled. "I want to see you."

Bennett raised his arms, and Cris pulled it over Bennett's head. The gray undershirt swiftly followed, exposing a broad chest liberally covered with dark fur. Cris combed his fingers through the hair and rubbed the pads of his thumbs over the dark nipples.

Bennett gasped and placed his palms against the wall. "Am I the only one getting naked?"

"You've seen me naked already," Cris pointed out. "I want to see all of you now." He brushed the back of his hand against the bulge in Bennett's pants, and Bennett shuddered. Cris smiled, slipped his fingers inside the waistband, and watched the muscles ripple again. Then he knelt at Bennett's feet to unlace his boots.

Bennett ran a hand through Cris's hair. "I like seeing you at my feet."

Cris grinned up at him. "I like the view too." He pulled Bennett's boots off and tugged down his pants and briefs. Oh yeah, he loved the sight of Bennett's half-hard dick against his strong, lightly furred thighs. Bennett's face was flushed, his eyes half-lidded as he looked down. Cris discarded the clothes and then cupped Bennett's ass so he could nuzzle into the curls framing his cock.

"You're a tease," Bennett hissed.

"You've just worked that out?" Cris licked his shaft from base to tip and swirled his tongue around the slit, loving the salty, bitter taste.

Bennett gave a strangled groan and tugged painfully at Cris's hair. "More."

Cris obliged and spent more time around the head. Each lick drew a fresh moan, so he sucked lightly on the head, and cupped the soft sac as he licked and nibbled down the shaft.

"It's going to be all over if we carry on like this," Bennett murmured.

"You come when you're ready, baby." Cris was prepared to wait for his release. He was only focused on Bennett and Bennett's pleasure.

"You're amazing, Lionman."

"Cris," he corrected. "I'm Lionman on stage."

"Cris," Bennett agreed on a slow breath. "Sorry. Suck me."

"Put your hands against the wall."

Cris waited until Bennett obeyed. Then he wrapped his hand around the shaft and relished the heavy weight against his palm. He rolled his balls in the other hand, and then he sucked in the head. Bennett groaned, but his hands stayed against the wall. Cris had a gag reflex and could only take in so much, but he used his hands as well as his tongue to drive Bennett mad. He sucked until Bennett cried out and bent over him as salty bursts pulsed down Cris's throat. They stayed in that position until Bennett softened in his mouth. Then

Bennett joined Cris on the floor as though his legs could no longer hold him up.

"Okay?" Cris asked, as he stroked Bennett's jaw.

Bennett gave a short laugh and hauled Cris in for an openmouthed kiss, his hand around the nape of Cris's neck and their tongues dueling together. Then Bennett rested his head on Cris's shoulder and pressed soft kisses into Cris's neck. They stayed there for a long time, neither of them anxious to move until Bennett sighed and raised his head. He looked the most relaxed Cris had ever seen. The more Cris loved on him, the more his pinched look eased. Cris intended to erase that look forever. "Damn."

Cris grinned at his lack of words. "Damn good?"

"Hell yes." Bennett brushed his lips over Cris's. "But what about you?"

"I thought we could go to bed." Cris had plans for Bennett, but they involved a soft mattress rather than a hard floor, so Cris stood and pulled Bennett to his feet.

Bennett groaned and rolled his shoulders. "I'm too old for wall sex."

"You weren't complaining a few minutes ago," Cris pointed out. He didn't care what Bennett was doing if he could watch Bennett's muscles rippling. He was a walking work of art. Maybe he should be doing a nude study of Bennett. His lips twitched. Bennett's head would explode if he suggested that.

"A few minutes ago, your mouth was wrapped around my dick. I couldn't speak, let alone complain."

"I'll have to remember that. Blowjobs melt your brain. As for being old"—Cris dug his fingers in Bennett's ribs, smirking as he yelped—"you're not that much older than me, dipshit."

"Nice," Bennett grumbled, pushed away Cris's fingers, and rubbed the sore spot. "Insults and assaults."

Cris stopped his complaints with a kiss and a roll of his hips against Bennett's. "Shut up and come to bed."

He grabbed Bennett's hand and tugged him to his bedroom. It was a mess, and at some point, he'd really have to change his sheets, but he pushed Bennett onto the bed, kicked off his shoes, and climbed on top of him. Bennett made him toppy and dominant in a way he hadn't been with other guys. He wanted to make Bennett forget his own name. From the way Bennett lay back on the pillows and waited for Cris to decide what to do, he had no objection.

Cris looked at Bennett's full and plump mouth. "I want to kiss you."

"Are you gonna get naked?"

"Soon. I want to kiss you first."

Bennett wrapped his arms around Cris's neck. "Then do it."

Cris bent forward, stretched out over Bennett's naked body, and brushed a light kiss over his lips.

"Tease," Bennett muttered.

"You think I'm teasing you? What about this?"

Cris deepened the kiss, and Bennett's mouth opened under his. He slid his tongue into Bennett's mouth and lazily they dueled, tongue around tongue. Cris kept kissing Bennett until Bennett thrust up against him, his hardening shaft trapped between them.

Cris sat back up on Bennett's thighs, swept his hands down Bennett's torso, and lightly pinched his nipples as his own dick jumped at Bennett's hiss.

"Get naked," Bennett ordered.

Cris pulled off his long-sleeve T-shirt, and Bennett's eyes darkened at the sight of his chest. When Cris scrambled off to get rid of his jeans and briefs, his dick slapped against his belly and left a sticky precome trail.

Bennett held out his hand. "Need you now."

Cris was back on the bed in seconds, stretched out over Bennett, skin against skin, hard cock touching hard cock, sweat and soft hair tickling Cris's body. He cradled Bennett's face with his hands. "You feel so good."

Bennett pressed a kiss into Cris's hand. "You'll feel even better inside me."

"I'm gonna have to teach you patience." Cris kissed Bennett, rolled off him, and leaned over to pull a condom and lube out of the drawer of the nightstand.

Bennett pulled his legs up to his chest, exposing his dark pink hole. Cris took in a deep breath because it would be damned embarrassing if he came before he'd had a chance to sample his lover.

He bent and licked a stripe from Bennett's balls to his hole. Then he squeezed lube onto his fingers. He didn't know how long it had been since Bennett had taken a cock, but there was no rush at all. Cris circled the muscle with the lube and waited until Bennett pushed against his fingers. Then he pressed one fingertip in.

"More," Bennett moaned.

He pressed in up to the knuckle, and Bennett's tight channel closed around him. Cris took his time and made sure Bennett could accept one finger before he went for a second.

Bennett grabbed his wrist. "I'm not a damned virgin. Fuck me!"

Cris figured the man knew his own body. He ripped open the condom packet and smoothed the rubber down his shaft. Then he leaned over Bennett and closed his eyes as he pressed into his tight hot glove. He waited until the tight look on Bennett's face eased, took a deep breath, and started to thrust. Bennett rested his legs over Cris's shoulders and let Cris do the work. When Cris wrapped his hand around Bennett's leaking shaft, Bennett's eyes fluttered shut and he moaned, and Cris couldn't take his gaze away from him. He pulled Bennett closer to him, and the change in position made Bennett gasp.

Sweat beading across his brow, Bennett opened his eyes and stared at Cris. "Fuck me harder."

Cris took his time, sped up his gentle thrusts, and changed his rhythm until Bennett was lost in his pleasure and begging Cris for more. Cris gritted his teeth and hung on to his control for as long as he could, but watching Bennett, being sheathed by his channel, was more than he could take. Sweat trickled down his spine as he gasped out, "Gonna come."

Bennett nodded and tensed his jaw as Cris jacked his cock. He grunted, thrust up through the tight channel of Cris's fingers, and spurted over them. Cris wiped his hand on the sheet, concentrated on thrusting harder until his balls tightened, and yelled out his pleasure as he came. Then he collapsed over Bennett's body, a breathless, sweaty mess.

It took a moment to unravel their limbs. Cris disposed of the condom in the trash can, and then he and Bennett folded into each other's arms and entwined their legs. Bennett made sleepy, contented noises against Cris's neck, and Cris smiled—his man was a snuggler. He shouldn't have been surprised.

When Bennett's breathing softened, Cris thought he was asleep, until he said, "I should go home."

Cris made a disapproving noise in the back of his throat and held Bennett closer. "It's snowing. They shut down the subway. You stay here where it's nice and warm."

"You don't mind?"

"I don't mind at all." Cris rolled so Bennett was effectively pinned to the bed. "Go to sleep, baby."

"Not your baby," Bennett muttered, but it didn't sound heated.

Cris was too tired to argue. He pushed a curl of Bennett's hair away from his eyes, and Bennett grumbled, but he was asleep between one breath and the next and making little snorting sounds. Cris took longer because he needed time to unwind, but eventually he fell into a dreamless sleep in Bennett's arms.

CRIS WOKE in the night to use the bathroom. By the time he returned, Bennett had rolled into the middle of the bed and spread out.

"Bed hogger," Cris whispered in Bennett's ear as he nudged him over.

Bennett mumbled something and rolled over, giving Cris fractionally more space.

Cris blinked. "Did you say you like kissing lions?" When he got no answer, he shook his head and settled down behind Bennett, who flinched and tried to pull away.

"Cold."

Cris wrapped an arm around him. "I know. You can warm me up."

"Lions furry."

Cris snickered. "You're the furry one."

Bennett snorted and fell asleep again.

THE NEXT time Cris woke, the world outside was nothing more than a sea of white. Snowstorms were forecast for most of the day. As Cris filled his coffee maker with water, Dan texted him to say he didn't need to come in. Cris put the phone down and hoped the bad weather didn't continue. He couldn't afford to lose too many shifts—his rent was due later in the month.

Bennett shuffled into the kitchen wearing just his jeans. "Is everything okay?"

"My shift at the bar is canceled."

"Yeah, we're closed too." Bennett narrowed his eyes. "You don't look happy about a snow day. Don't you like crashing out on the sofa and watching your DVDs?"

"Yeah, when I'm not worrying about making the rent. I'm gonna need to find an extra job soon." Cris sighed and tugged Bennett in for a kiss. "I'm sorry. My money woes are not your problem. Did you sleep all right?"

Bennett didn't look happy, but he obliged with a kiss. "Coffee?"

"I can do that."

They ended up on the sofa as entwined as they had been in bed with Bennett snuggled against Cris's chest as they sipped coffee. Cris felt better as the caffeine spread through his system.

Bennett raised his head. "You know I could loan you your rent."

Cris pressed his lips to Bennett's mouth. "I know. Thank you. But we're not at that stage yet."

"Okay." Bennett nodded his head. "But the offer's there." He rested his head back on Cris's chest.

Cris sighed. "It's a snow day. I have food. We're not going anywhere. What should we watch?"

"*Whiteout, Frozen, Eight Below?*"

"Ha-ha. I have them all. Which one do you want to watch?"

"You pick one." Bennett got to his feet. "I'll get dressed. My jeans are still damp from yesterday."

"You can take sweats and a hoodie or a long-sleeve T-shirt from my closet."

"Thanks."

Cris was still choosing a movie when he heard a strangled gasp behind him. He wandered curiously into his bedroom to find Bennett staring wide-eyed into his closet. "Is everything okay?"

"I...." Bennett pointed at his costumes.

"Yeah, I have more costumes than clothes."

"I've never seen anything like it."

"Aw, are you saying I'm unique?" Cris rested his chin on Bennett's shoulder. "Everything else is on this side."

Bennett raised a hand to pat Cris's cheek. "I can think a lot of words to call you. Unique is one of them."

"Thanks, I think."

Cris moved around Bennett and pulled out two pairs of sweatpants and two hoodies. "Do you need socks?"

"Please."

He handed Bennett a pair of thick woolen socks. "My mom bought me these. She thinks I don't dress warmly enough."

"Do you ever wear them?"

"Only in here."

They got dressed again and settled back to watch movies for the whole day. Cris was used to watching movies, but having Bennett there made a welcome change, especially when Bennett leaned against him, Cris wrapped his arm around Bennett, and they forgot about the outside world as they snuggled together.

CHAPTER 16

"IT'S YOURS." Cris held out Bennett's phone as he walked into the kitchen. "I'll make us some coffee."

"Thanks. Hello?" Bennett answered the phone, most of his attention on an article he was reading on his iPad. "Hi, Mama. No busier than usual. Just looking at potential land Tata might be interested in. I'll email it later."

Cris rolled his eyes. He was going to make it his mission in life to make Bennett take some downtime, and Bennett had told him he was watching stupid videos on YouTube. The man never switched off. After two months together, Cris had realized his boyfriend—they'd both stopped hyperventilating over that word now—never stopped living and breathing the family business.

"Does it have to be today? I'm busy. Yes, I know I said that, but I'm busy later."

Cris frowned. As far as he knew, both of them were free all day. They'd made a tentative plan to see a movie and go for Thai food, but that was all. He heard a clatter behind him and turned his head to see Bennett righting a mug he'd knocked over. The color had drained out of Bennett's face, and Cris was worried he was about to pass out.

"You okay, Bennett?" he murmured, not wanting to disturb the conversation.

Bennett held up his hand and spoke into the phone. "Mama, it's not really a good time."

He listened for a long time with a resigned look on his face. Cris wanted to go over and stroke his back, offer him some form of comfort, but every pore of Bennett was radiating "don't come the hell near me." Cris leaned against the kitchen counter and waited patiently until the call was over.

"Okay, I'll come, and Mikey too if he's free. Yes. It'll be good to see you and Tata. I'm going to bring a friend with me. No, not a girlfriend. He's...."

Bennett stared at Cris who mouthed, "It's okay."

"He's a good friend of mine. I want you to meet him." Bennett smiled at Cris. "I'll tell Mikey. I've got to go, Mama."

He disconnected the call and stared at Cris, his eyes comically wide. "What the hell have I just done?"

"I think you just invited me to meet the parents."

"I repeat, what the hell have I just done?"

Cris batted his eyelashes. "Aw, honey, does this mean you've met the right woman?" His smile faded when Bennett didn't laugh. "Bennett? You don't have to take me. I won't be offended."

Bennett shook his head. "Yes, I do. I want to take you. I want to tell them about us."

Cris took both of Bennett's hands in his. "I'll be by your side."

"What if I turn out to be another Petrovski screwup?"

Cris shrugged. "Never gonna happen. I love this Petrovski."

"I love you too."

IT WAS obvious to Cris that Bennett was freaking out and trying his best to show how calm he was. His face was pinched and his glorious eyes dull. Cris appreciated the effort, but he'd have preferred Bennett to come to him for comfort. They were a minute from leaving Cris's apartment to go visit Bennett's parents, but Cris wasn't letting Bennett go anywhere until they talked. He grabbed Bennett by the biceps and forced him to look at him. It was the one time he really appreciated being the same height, because Bennett found it hard to look away.

"We don't have to do this now," Cris said, his voice calm and soothing. "We don't have to do this at all. My love for you is not conditional on you telling your parents."

"I know," Bennett said. "But my love for you is conditional on being honest and open about our relationship. You've been nothing but honest with me, and I owe you the same."

"Some couples never tell their parents about their relationship, and I get that. Sometimes it's easier to keep quiet. You don't have to tell them today. I'm not walking out the door if you decide to keep quiet."

Bennett licked his lips, and Cris could see the fear behind his eyes. But there was more than fear. There was also determination. "Thank you for telling me that. I needed to hear it, but I'm not just doing this for us. I'm doing this for Mikey as well. He needs to see he's got a big brother who has his back no matter what."

As Mikey had bailed on the meal once he found out what Bennett was going to do, Cris thought it was irrelevant, but he didn't say that to Bennett.

"Mikey knows you've got his back," Cris said. "You don't need to give him some big declaration."

"*I* tried the big declaration," Bennett muttered. "He told me not to be such a girl."

"How the heck does your sister let you get away with comments like that?" Cris shuddered, imagining the reaction if he'd made a "like a girl" comment in front of his own family.

"He's not stupid enough to say it in front of her," Bennett pointed out. "Hannah would shred him limb from limb."

Cris could imagine Mikey's reaction to Bennett being emotional, but he was having a hard time trying to imagine Bennett *being* emotional. Bennett was not a "hearts and flowers" type of guy. He showed his love in different ways, from repairing the faucet that Cris had been meaning to fix and never had, to collecting Cris from Cowboys and Angels every night even if he had to go to work a few hours later. It didn't matter how many times Cris told him he was fine to come home by himself. Bennett was there outside the bar with a warm car and a hot drink. His guy was pretty damned perfect really.

Cris looked into Bennett's eyes. "Take a few deep breaths. You won't help yourself or Mikey if you pass out now."

"I'm not that flaky."

Cris grinned at the snap in Bennett's voice. That was more like it. "Come on, then, or your mother will be calling to find out where we are."

"She's already called three times," Bennett grimaced as he confessed. "I switched my phone off. The woman is nothing if not persistent."

"Let's get going then before she turns up on your doorstep." Cris held out his gloved hand to Bennett. "I've got your back."

Bennett tugged Cris in for a quick kiss and then let go. "Likewise, lover."

"You might not want to call me that in front of your parents," Cris suggested. "Not unless I can call you *baby*."

"Isn't going to happen," Bennett said flatly.

"Sweet cheeks? Pumpkin? Loverboy?"

"I'll end you right now."

Cris grinned at him. "Feeling better?"

"Yes. I hate you."

"I know you do." Cris drew Bennett into a longer kiss. When he raised his head, Bennett's eyes were closed and his lips soft and red. If they hadn't been going somewhere, Cris would have taken him back to bed.

MRS. PETROVSKI was a smaller version of the two boys, although her hair was almost gray and in a neat pixie cut. She wasn't quite what Cris expected. He realized he'd had some idea of a Hollywood Eastern European matriarch, and instead what he got was an immaculately dressed New Yorker.

"Benny, I was starting to get worried. And this is your friend?"

She looked puzzled as she studied Cris, but she hugged her son until he protested that he couldn't breathe. Then it was his turn, and Cris flailed a moment before he hugged her back. She flushed and fluttered a moment and then invited them into the kitchen. Cris could see immediately that the kitchen was the heart of the home. It was about three times the size of Cris's entire home and more like an industrial kitchen with an oversize oven and appliances. Just off the kitchen was a room with a table set for dining. The table was large enough for twelve.

Mr. Petrovski sat at a breakfast bar, reading a newspaper. He put it down and peered over his glasses at the new arrivals. When he got to his feet, Cris could see he was barely an inch shorter than his son, but Cris knew exactly what Bennett would look like when he was older. He hugged Bennett and shook Cris's hand.

The welcome was much more than Cris expected, yet Bennett had said his parents were good people. He really hoped the warmth was still intact by the end of the visit. It would be a tragedy to fracture this loving family. He wondered idly when he'd introduce Bennett to his own parents and siblings. They knew about him, of course, but Cris had been so involved with Bennett that he hadn't made it over to the family home.

Mr. Petrovski offered them beer, and when they were settled, Bennett said, "Who else is coming for dinner, Mama?"

"I've invited your sister and Adam for lunch," Mrs. Petrovski said.

Cris felt the tension flood through Bennett. It was one thing to have this conversation with his parents, but adding his sister and brother-in-law just increased the tension. Cris brushed Bennett's leg with his, Bennett stiffened but he didn't pull away.

"I thought Hannah was away this weekend," Bennett said.

"Her in-laws canceled. Betty's got the flu. I thought it'd be wonderful to have you all together." Mrs. Petrovski beamed at them, but her smile faded at the tight expression on her son's face. "What's the issue?"

Bennett shook his head. "Nothing. It's okay, Mama."

"Then why do you look like I've just killed your puppy?"

"You never allowed us to have a dog." Bennett smiled, but Cris could see it was a struggle, and from the frown on Mrs. Petrovski's face, she could see it too.

Bennett glanced at Cris, who gave him the most reassuring smile he could manage.

"What's the matter?" she demanded as she reached out for Bennett's hands. "Talk to me. You're scaring me now, Benny."

Bennett grasped her hands, clearly unable to force out the words. The silence in the kitchen was deafening, and the sudden sound of the doorbell was both a welcome relief and an annoying distraction. Mrs. Petrovski bustled away to open the door, and Cris heard the enthusiastic welcome as she greeted her daughter and son-in-law. Bennett stared at some unknown point in the distance, and Cris waited patiently for him to focus again. The only person who seemed oblivious to the tension was Mr. Petrovski, who'd returned to reading the sports section of his newspaper.

Watching Bennett and Hannah hug in the middle of the kitchen, Cris could see they were all cut from the same mold. Hannah was nearly as tall as her brother, although thankfully, she wasn't built with the same broad shoulders, and her dark hair curled around her ears just like Bennett's. From the scolding she gave him, it had been some time since she'd seen her brother. Bennett had that "deer trapped in headlights" expression as she pointed out what useless brothers she had, and she included Mikey in the tirade even though he wasn't there. It was equally obvious they were all very fond of each other, and Cris could see why Bennett had fought so hard not to destroy the family balance.

Then Hannah turned her attention on Cris. From the smirk on Bennett's face, Cris wore the same trapped expression.

"Who are you? I haven't met you before."

Mrs. Petrovski intervened before any of the men could speak. "This is Cris, Benny's friend."

Cris shook her hand and then her husband's. Adam was thirtyish and stocky, with sandy-colored hair and startling light-blue eyes. He seemed familiar, although Cris couldn't work out why until Adam said, "I've seen you at Cowboys and Angels. You're Dan's friend."

"Yeah, that's right. I thought I recognized you."

If Adam knew he was a friend of Dan's, then he probably knew Cris was gay. And if he knew Cris was gay.... From his pensive expression, the same thought had occurred to Bennett.

"Did you make pierogies?" Hannah asked. "And kielbasa?"

"Yes, yes, and golabki for Benny. Don't worry all your favorite dishes are here."

Bennett kissed her cheek. "You're the best, Mama."

She beamed at him, and thankfully she didn't pursue her questions as she bustled away to serve dinner.

Cris sat next to Bennett at the table, Bennett's leg pushed up against his. Hannah and Adam sat opposite them, and they kept up a steady conversation about Cowboys and Angels. Adam and Bennett had been customers of the bar for years and had a stream of stories, mainly about Gideon and Ariel. Cris choked at Adam's description of Dan's reaction to Ariel knocking over a stack of glasses when she was playing baseball with Luis in the bar.

Adam wiped the tears from his eyes. "I thought Dan was gonna kill her."

"If Gideon hadn't been between them, I think Dan would have tried," Bennett agreed.

Cris chuckled. "When was this?"

"A couple of years ago," Adam said. "Before they... uh... became family. But she had a dead shot."

"The girl has a mean aim," Bennett agreed.

Mrs. Petrovski sniffed. "That girl needs a good spanking."

"She's a bit old for a spanking, Mama," Adam said. "She's working now."

She sniffed again. "No one is too old for a spanking."

Bennett pressed closer to Cris, who took that to mean Mrs. Petrovski practiced what she preached. He wanted to put an arm around Bennett, but he couldn't, so he sat as close as he could and tried to project soothing thoughts to him.

The food was out of this world. Cris ate everything on his plate and more besides. He was going to have to work his butt off in the gym or he'd never be able to strip again.

"You're the best cook I've ever met, Mrs. Petrovski." He rubbed his belly. "Much better than my mom, but don't tell her I said that."

She beamed at him. "Call me Mama. Everyone does."

"You've just found the way into my parents' good books," Hannah said. "They never like people who turned their nose up at Polish food."

"Anyone who does that is an idiot," Cris declared.

"For a man in your profession, you eat a lot of food," Hannah said.

"What do you do?" Tata asked.

Cris looked at Bennett, who gave a tiny shrug. "I'm working at Cowboys and Angels as a bartender. Before that I was a stripper at Forbidden Nightz."

The silence was deafening. Cris could feel Bennett shrinking beside him. He expected to be shown the door, but to his surprise, Mr. Petrovski nodded. "I hear Lionman is very successful."

How did Bennett's father know he was the Lionman? Was he having him followed? Cris bit his lip, but he couldn't downplay his career choice just because it was unconventional.

"Yeah, I was successful. I had a lot of fun doing it. I hope I will again."

"You should always do something you're good at," Mr. Petrovski said and calmly asked his wife for cream.

Cris could see the startled looks being exchanged between Bennett, Hannah, and Adam. That obviously wasn't what they expected from their father.

"I like working at Cowboys and Angels too. It's a good place to work."

Mr. Petrovski inclined his head. "Gideon is a fine man and a successful businessman. I don't know his... new manager but I've heard good things about him."

"How long have you known Gideon?"

"I knew Gideon and Sarah when they first moved into the bar. It was a tragedy what happened to her and their boy. What was his name?"

"Simon," Bennett supplied.

Mr. Petrovski nodded. "Simon. He was far too young to be taken in such a dreadful manner."

Cris watched as he made the sign of the cross and the family, apart from Adam, joined in. It was the first time he'd seen an overtly religious sign from Bennett, and it unsettled him. Cris's family weren't religious, and Cris called himself a "lapsed anything" when pressed. He freely admitted he was uncomfortable around religion, but then, religion was uncomfortable around him. If he was going to spend time around the Petrovskis, he would have to suck it up and get on with it. Adam didn't seem concerned. *Be like Adam.* He had a feeling he would be saying that a lot.

"It's a shame Mikey couldn't join us," Mrs. Petrovski said after a moment's silence. "It's been too long since we were all together as a family."

Hannah rolled her eyes. "It's been two weeks, Mama. We were all here for your birthday, remember?"

Mrs. Petrovski made a shushing noise. "When's he going to set a date with Julianne? It's time that boy was wed."

Cris felt Bennett stiffen beside him as tension flooded through his muscles. Taking a chance he placed one hand on Bennett's thigh, intending just to give a quick squeeze. To his surprise, Bennett grabbed his hand and kept it there.

"Maybe he's having second thoughts," Hannah said.

"It's time he got over that," Mrs. Petrovski said brusquely. "He's making Julianne unhappy with his delays and distractions."

"He shouldn't get married unless he's absolutely sure," Bennett said.

Mrs. Petrovski shook her head. "No one is sure until they've walked down the aisle. I wasn't sure what I was doing until the moment I saw your father standing at the altar." She patted her husband's hand.

He smiled at her. "You were a vision, my dear."

"Oh Mama, Mikey's just trying to convince himself marriage is what he wants," Hannah said. "If he gets married, he'll be divorced within a year."

"Hannah!"

Over Mrs. Petrovski's horrified exclamation, Cris stared at Hannah, who caught his gaze and gave the briefest of nods. He realized she knew. She knew about Mikey, and she knew about Bennett. If she knew, Adam probably did too.

Bennett shivered beside him, and Cris squeezed his hand again. Bennett squeezed back and tugged his hand free. Then he took a deep breath and said, "Mama, Tata, there's something I need to tell you."

They both looked at him expectantly, and Bennett opened his mouth, but the words seemed to dry in his throat.

"What is it, dear?" Mrs. Petrovski asked.

The heavy food sat like a lead weight in Cris's stomach as he braced himself for whatever was going to come next.

"I should have told you a long time ago, but…." Bennett took a drink of water. "I'm gay. Cris isn't my friend. Well, he is my friend, but—"

"He's your boyfriend," Hannah butted in.

Cris didn't know whether to thank her or throttle her. Even in something as important as this, a Petrovski sibling had to muscle in.

"He's my boyfriend," Bennett said quietly as though Hannah hadn't spoken, and he took Cris's hand and entwined their fingers for everyone to see.

Aside from a gasp from Mrs. Petrovski, the silence around the table was deafening.

CHAPTER 17

IN THE silence Cris was acutely conscious of Bennett sitting next to him. Bennett hadn't drawn a breath since his last word, and every muscle was rigid. Bennett was clearly waiting for disaster to fall upon his head. It didn't take long to oblige.

"Don't say such ridiculous things, Benny. You're not that way. You just haven't found the right girl." Mrs. Petrovski frowned as though Bennett had announced he was Santa Claus.

Hannah snorted. "Mama, believe me, he's never going to find the right girl. He only said that to keep you off his back."

Bennett stared at her, and Cris realized he'd thought his sister was unaware of his sexual orientation.

The color drained from Mrs. Petrovski's face. "Don't you dare say that about your brother. Benny's not a homosexual. He can't be. It's a mortal sin."

"Mama—" Bennett started, his face white. He had a death grip on Cris's hand.

She turned on him fiercely. "Be quiet. We'll talk to Father Michael. He can find you help. There are programs that can make you right—"

Bennett straightened up, his face resolute. "They don't work, Mama. You can't fix being gay. It doesn't work like that."

"You don't know that," she insisted. "You're broken. You need help."

"Mama, stop!" Mr. Petrovski shocked them all with his quiet order. She swung round, but he held up his hand. "There's nothing wrong with Bennett."

Cris wanted to hold him, but Bennett's grip was painfully tight, and there was nothing he could do except ride out the storm and hope they were both intact at the end.

She stared at her husband, a betrayed look on her face. "Tata, you heard what he said."

"I heard, and it doesn't change anything."

"God—"

"Loves Bennett just as surely as he loves you. Mama, Bennett isn't a broken watch. He doesn't need to be taken apart and fixed. Those programs do more damage than they help." A slight flush of color stained his weathered cheeks.

Bennett stiffened, and Cris processed what he'd said. Why had Bennett's father investigated reparative therapy programs? Did he know about Bennett? Did he know about Mikey?

"You don't know that," she insisted.

"I do."

"We can find something else, a counselor or a doctor," she said desperately. "Father Michael will know someone who can help."

"Mama," Bennett started, but she turned away from him, and Bennett made a noise like he was holding back a sob.

Cris decided to intervene. "I think we should go."

She stared across at him as though seeing him for the first time, and her eyes went flat and bitter. "You made him like this. You turned my son away from the right path. You're a whore. Get out of my house."

"Cris is no whore, and if he goes, I go," Bennett warned. He was pale and pinched and two spots blazed on his cheeks.

She nodded. "We don't need your filth in our house. You go and don't come back until you're ready to repent."

"If Bennett leaves, so do we," Hannah declared.

Mrs. Petrovski looked genuinely shocked. "Hannah Zofia Petrovski—"

Hannah shook her head. "Bellingham. My name is Hannah Bellingham, and Bennett is my brother."

Adam looked as though he wanted to be anywhere except at that table, but Hannah's expression was fierce.

"Quiet, all of you. No one is going anywhere," Mr. Petrovski barked.

Bennett collapsed into Cris, who put his arm around him, ignoring Mrs. Petrovski's scowl. Hannah sat back after a quick touch on her arm from Adam.

Mr. Petrovski looked at Bennett. "Your mother is upset. You've sprung this news on her, and you have to give her a chance to understand."

"There's nothing to understand," his wife said, but they all ignored her.

"He's not staying here to be abused," Cris said fiercely.

Mr. Petrovski glanced at him, and to Cris's surprise, nodded approvingly. "You stand by my son."

"I won't let you destroy him," Cris warned. "He's done what you wanted for all his life. You're building a family empire. Did you ever think about what he wanted? That he might not want to carry on the family business?" Cris ignored Bennett's gasp.

"He's never complained," Mr. Petrovski said.

"Of course he didn't. He's been so busy trying to be the good son, the big brother, the heir to the empire. Bennett's wearing himself to the bone and concealing the fact that he's gay in case you reject him. It turns out he was right to be worried."

It was a dramatic thing to say over the remains of a family dinner, but Cris meant every word.

"Bennett is a good son," Mr. Petrovski agreed.

"And the best big brother." Hannah cast a fond glance at Bennett.

Mrs. Petrovski said nothing. She sat with her arms folded and glared at Cris, who scowled right back. The svelte New Yorker had been replaced by the matriarch. Cris didn't care.

Cris turned to Bennett. "I'm going to take you home now."

The muscle in Bennett's jaw jumped, and Cris could see he was holding on to his control with effort. He gave a curt nod and got to his feet. Cris stood and was about to lead him from the table when Mr. Petrovski spoke.

"Sit down, son. We need to talk."

Cris put his arm around Bennett. "You can talk another time."

"No, Cris, please." Bennett smiled wanly at him. "Let's get it over with."

They sat and waited for Bennett's father to speak, and he took his time, but finally he said, "You have a fine young man here, Bennett."

"I know."

Mr. Petrovski sighed. "No parent likes to be faced with the fact they've failed their child."

"You haven't failed me," Bennett protested.

"I haven't considered you, have I? You—or Michaś."

Cris narrowed his eyes. The old man seemed to be talking about one thing, but Cris was sure he was talking about something else.

"We both want to make you happy," Bennett said.

"But not at the expense of your happiness." Mr. Petrovski fixed his gaze on Bennett. "You should have told me."

"Yes, sir."

"This is why Mikey is doing stupid things like picking fights?" Bennett nodded.

"I'm going to talk to Mikey. It's time he faced up to reality."

"What are you going to say to him?" Bennett asked. "He can't take much more at the moment."

"Nonsense, Mikey's a strong boy," Mrs. Petrovski said.

"No, Mama, he really isn't," Hannah snapped. "He needs a good spanking."

Mrs. Petrovski glowered at her daughter. "At least he knows what's right. He's found a good woman to spend the rest of his life with."

Hannah burst out laughing. "You have to be joking. You can't be that blind."

"Hannah." Mr. Petrovski fixed his daughter with a frown. "Apologize to your mother."

Hannah pressed her lips together. "I'm sorry, Mama."

Mrs. Petrovski looked visibly upset. "Why would you say that to me?"

Hannah ran her hands through her hair. "Mama—"

"Hannah, don't," Bennett said. "It's not fair on Mikey. He's not here."

"I will have this conversation with Michaś and with Mama," Mr. Petrovski said firmly. "It's not your concern."

"He's my brother. Of course he's my concern. Just like Benny's my concern."

Cris's admiration of Hannah was growing by the second. He'd been resentful that she seemed to escape the family pressure that had been put upon Bennett, but he could see she was a fierce defender of her brothers.

"Thanks, sis," Bennett murmured.

Hannah leaned into Adam, who hugged her closely. She looked tired—much like Bennett at that moment.

Mr. Petrovski turned to his wife. "Mama, let's have coffee and we can all calm down."

Her face was pinched and pale, but she nodded, rose, and took some of the empty dishes with her. Cris stood and carried two of the larger bowls to the sink. She didn't look pleased to receive his assistance, but she muttered her thanks. Mr. Petrovski nodded approvingly at Cris. At least someone appreciated him.

Conversation over coffee turned to business as Hannah asked Bennett about the progress of the housing project. Bennett made an effort to pull his control around him and told her about his issues with local plumbers. And Mrs. Petrovski sat in stony silence scowling at all of them and ignoring any attempt to pull her into the conversation. Cris discovered both Adam and Hannah worked for Petrovski in different departments. He listened to the conversation with half an ear, his main focus on Bennett, ready to intervene if necessary.

"Cris, your help please."

To his surprise—and everyone else's, judging by the sudden silence—Mrs. Petrovski spoke directly to him.

"Yes, ma'am." Cris decided not to chance calling her Mama, and she didn't correct him.

He followed her into the kitchen and waited as she filled the sink with hot, soapy water.

"I'll load the dishwasher. You can wash the big dishes. They have to be washed by hand."

Because they worked in silence apart from occasional direction from Mrs. Petrovski, Cris could hear the low murmur of conversation around the table. He relaxed when he heard Bennett's rumble of laughter.

"How did you meet my son?" Mrs. Petrovski asked suddenly.

"I took Mikey home when he… wasn't very well. Bennett was waiting for him."

Her hands tightened around a dishcloth. "You mean Mikey had too much to drink?"

"Yes."

"He drinks too much."

Cris stayed quiet, not wanting to pursue the reasons for Mikey's liquor habit.

Mrs. Petrovski sighed as she put down the cloth. "Come with me."

He followed her out of the kitchen and into a large living area, stylishly decorated in cream with turquoise accents. Mrs. Petrovski closed the door, and Cris looked at her in alarm. But when she pointed at a sofa, he sat obediently. She took a large wingback chair opposite him and sat bolt upright, her legs neatly crossed at the ankles.

Cris waited. If she thought separating him from the herd was going to make him cower, she had another think coming.

Finally she spoke. "I'm not blind. Nor am I stupid, whatever my daughter thinks."

"I'm sure she doesn't—"

He stopped when she held up a hand.

"I've known something was wrong with both my sons for a long time."

Cris bristled. "There is nothing *wrong* with them."

Her lip curled. "From *your* perspective I imagine not. However, I'm their mother."

"And what has changed?" Cris asked heatedly. "You have two loving sons who work in the family business and love their parents enough to give up their hopes and dreams. What the hell—" He cut himself off with a snap. "You should count yourself lucky you have sons who care."

"I do. I did," she said pointedly.

"Until today?"

She inclined her head.

It was Cris's turn to curl his lip. "Ma'am, if you reject your sons for who they love, then you're a fool."

It suddenly occurred to him he'd just openly admitted Mikey was gay or bi.

Her scowl deepened. "It's a sin. It's wrong."

Cris mentally thanked his parents for never dragging him down this road. He took a deep breath and tried again. "They're your sons, and they love you. But Mikey's on the point of doing something really stupid, and if you're not careful, he's going to end up in prison or… the morgue."

Color drained from Mrs. Petrovski's face so suddenly Cris was certain she was going to pass out. "That's not true."

"It is true, and Bennett is tearing himself apart to keep him together. I love your son, and I'm going to look after him whether you like it or not. I don't care if I never see you again, but you can't chase me out of your son's life."

She stared at him for a long while. "I will get Father Michael to pray for their immortal souls."

"Do what you like. I'll be taking care of Bennett's mind and body in this life."

There was a long pause, and then she said, "If you were a woman, you'd be everything I wanted in a daughter-in-law. You're fierce and loyal."

"I'm a man who's devoted to your son. Isn't that enough?"

"It's enough for me," Bennett said from the doorway. He looked pale but resolute. "Let's go home, Cris."

Without a backward look at Mrs. Petrovski, Cris joined him at the door to discover Hannah and Adam already there, putting on their coats.

"Do you need a ride?" Adam asked.

"We're fine," Cris said before Bennett could speak. He'd had enough family for one day, and he needed as much space as he could get from the Petrovskis.

Hannah gave him an understanding smile. "I'll call you, Benny." She wrapped her brother in a comforting hug, and Cris heard her whisper, "I've been waiting for this day for a long time."

"Me too," Bennett managed.

Cris shook hands with Adam and then turned to Bennett. Mr. Petrovski was nowhere to be seen. "Your father?"

"We said goodbye to him already. He wants to talk to you before we go. He's still in the kitchen."

Cris walked back into the kitchen to find Bennett's father staring into space. He looked ten years older than when they arrived.

"Sir?" Cris said gently.

Mr. Petrovski turned to look at him. "You've given me a lot to think about, Cris."

"I'm sorry if I spoke out of turn."

"You did, but it needed to be said. My boys should have been honest a long time ago."

"They love you and just wanted to make you happy."

"At the expense of their own happiness." Mr. Petrovski sighed.

Cris inclined his head. "What happens now?"

"Now, my wife and I need to have a long conversation."

Cris asked the one thing that had been puzzling him. "How did you know about the conversion programs?"

"Children always make the mistake of thinking their parents are oblivious to what is going on in their lives. I did some research when the boys were teenagers."

"You knew they were gay?"

"I suspected Mikey was. Then a good friend called me. He'd been talking to a young man in a laundromat who told him about his boyfriend, who had the same name as my eldest son."

Cris blinked. "The old guy."

Mr. Petrovski gave a wry smile. "The old guy. I never knew about Bennett until then."

"I had no idea." Cris had outed Bennett without even realizing it. Bennett would kill him.

"I love my sons."

"I can see that, sir."

If he'd kept their secret for that long, his love was fierce and protective. It was a shame he couldn't have talked to them about it before Mikey started to fall apart.

"My wife loves them too."

Cris kept quiet. He knew that she did, but her idea of love was alien to Cris. Mr. Petrovski gave him a wry smile.

"You take care of my son, and I'll take care of my wife."

"I won't let her hurt him," Cris warned.

"You're a good boy, but I know my wife. She needs time to think and process. You'll see. She'll see our sons are still good boys."

"Maybe you need to see them as men in their own right," Cris suggested.

Mr. Petrovski was silent for a moment. "Maybe we do, young man. Maybe we do. Give us time."

The conversation seemed to be over, so Cris said goodbye and rejoined the others in the hallway.

"What did Tata want?" Bennett asked as he helped Cris shrug on his jacket.

"I'll tell you later," Cris muttered.

He wasn't sure how Bennett was going to take the fact that he'd inadvertently outed him to his father.

Bennett looked at him curiously but dropped the subject. "Let's go home."

Cris had never heard a better suggestion.

Neither sibling seemed willing to engage with their mother, and they left the family home. When they got outside, they parted company with Hannah and Adam and Cris studied Bennett.

"What do you want to do now?"

Bennett shoved his hands into his jacket. "Can we go back to your place?"

"Yours is closer."

"That's why I want to go to yours."

"Only if you don't hog our bed," Cris teased.

"Our bed. I like that." Bennett gave his first smile since he told his parents his news, even if it didn't reach his eyes.

Cris was pleased to see it, but he was waiting for Bennett to fall apart, and he'd be ready to hold him together when he did.

"I like that too." Cris bumped him with his elbow. "You're still gonna steal all the space, aren't you?"

"I don't know what you're talking about," Bennett said haughtily.

"Sure you do. Space hogger."

Bennett snorted. "Snorer."

"You snore."

"I never snore."

"You always snore," Cris scoffed.

Bennett stopped and turned to Cris. "No one ever knew that before."

Cris wrinkled his brow. "Knew what?"

"That I snore or hog the bed. I've never shared a bed with anyone."

"You do now." One tear spilled over onto Bennett's cheek, and Cris wiped it away with his thumb. "Let's go home, baby. We can curl up in bed, and then you can fall apart."

Bennett didn't call him out on the endearment, and he didn't deny that he was going to fall to pieces.

Dear Reader,
By now, your Cock must be HORNY. So I am.
I wish I were with you to Suck your Cock.
How big is your Cock?

7"   8' ——— 10"?

I want you to Fuck me.

How does your CUM taste?
Sweet, bitter, Salty?

CHAPTER 18

CRIS BUNDLED Bennett through the door, stripped him down without ceremony, and hustled him under the bed covers. Then he did the same and climbed into bed, He wrapped his arms around Bennett, who let out a whisper of a sigh and pushed back against him. Cris rested one hand across Bennett's heart.

"Now you can let go," he whispered. "I've got you."

Bennett made a noise in the back of his throat, and then the dam broke. Sobs tore from his throat, loud in the silence of the bedroom. Cris did nothing but hold him. The storm passed as they all do, and finally Bennett relaxed against Cris.

"I'm sorry." He sounded worn beyond belief.

"Nothing to be sorry for," Cris said.

"I've brought you nothing but trouble."

Cris kissed the nape of Bennett's neck. "You, never, but your family needs work."

Bennett sighed as he turned in Cris's arms and buried his face against Cris's chest. "I'm exhausted."

"Then go to sleep. We can talk in the morning before work."

"I don't even know if I've got a job to go to in the morning."

Cris stroked Bennett's hair. "I think you have."

"Tata—"

"Already knew about you."

"I wondered, but he never said."

"He didn't throw you out tonight. He's not going to tomorrow. Your father may not like it, but he loves his boys."

"Mama—"

Cris sighed, turned onto his back, and tucked Bennett more comfortably against him. "She also knew. She just didn't want to admit it." Cris was never going to repeat the conversation he had with Mrs. Petrovski. Bennett didn't deserve that.

"Is that what she said?"

"More or less. She knows about Mikey too."

"I ought to warn him."

"No, this is between Mikey and your parents. Your dad will speak to him."

Bennett pressed a kiss into Cris's skin. "Why did you look so freaked when you came away from talking to my father?"

"Freaked? Oh, yeah. I've got a confession to make."

"Oh?"

"I kinda outed you."

"Huh? We'd already had that conversation. I told him, remember?"

"Not today. I met an old guy at the laundromat who watched me draw you. He showed me a photo of him and his husband, and I did a quick sketch for him. I never thought he might know you when I told him I was in love with you. It turns out he's a friend of your father's."

"I wonder who? Tata's never mentioned knowing any gay men."

"He didn't know the man was gay until that conversation. He was named Charles, and his partner was Pip—Philip."

"Uncle Charles? You've got to be mistaken. He was married to Auntie Pip. I never met her, but they were together a long time. He was devoted to her."

"Uh-huh." Cris let out a wealth of expression.

"Oh my God. Uncle Chuck is gay?" Bennett let out a bark of laughter. "Poor Tata. His world is turning upside down. I bet he hasn't told Mama."

"At least your dad is making the effort."

"Unlike Mama?"

"She's got a way to go yet," Cris said a touch grimly. He wasn't ready to forgive her for the way she'd treated her son.

"I thought it would be Tata who would lose his shit."

"In all fairness, your dad's had time to process his feelings. Your mom has just buried hers."

Bennett huddled closer to Cris. "Is it awful to say I can't take on her feelings too? I've spent so long trying to deal with mine and Mikey's. I need her to suck it up and deal."

Cris pressed a tender kiss into his hair. "It's human to want your parents to behave like the grown-ups in the arrangement. You don't have to take on her feelings too. That's what your dad is for."

"Poor Tata."

"Your sister is a tiger."

Bennett chuckled. "You don't want to get on the wrong side of Hannah. She could take down me and Mikey with one hand tied behind her back."

"She's got your back, though."

"I know. I'm very lucky."

Conversation trailed away, and Cris was almost asleep when Bennett said, "I've got you too."

He was too tired to do anything more than kiss Bennett, tumble into a warm, cozy sleep, and leave the world behind.

CRIS SAT up next to Bennett, heart pounding as someone did their level best to hammer their fist through the door.

"What the hell? Is there a fire?" Bennett stared at him, looking adorably sleepy and confused.

"This is déjà vu," Cris muttered. He climbed out of bed and pulled on the nearest sweats.

"What?"

"You'd better get dressed. I think this is Mikey."

This time Cris had the foresight to stand back before he answered the door and managed to avoid a fist in the face.

Mikey stormed in and pushed past Cris as though he were a mere triviality. "Bennett, where the hell are you?"

Bennett came out, looking sleepy and rumpled. "Mikey? What time is it?"

"Six a.m. What the hell happened yesterday?"

The fear on Bennett's face was plain to see, so Cris went to him and put an arm around his shoulders.

"What happened?" Bennett asked.

"I called Mama last night. She refused to take my call. Then I called Tata. He said he'd speak to me today. He wants me to go into the office at three."

The muscle twitched in Bennett's jaw. "I think you'd better sit down."

Mikey's expression hardened. "If you don't tell me what's going on, I'm going to friggin' kill you."

Cris stepped between Bennett and Mikey. "Sit the fuck down," he ordered.

Mikey huffed, but he threw himself onto the sofa. "I need coffee."

Cris stared at him a long time, and then Mikey reddened and said, "Please."

He nodded. "I'll make coffee."

Bennett frowned and said, "That's my phone."

He backtracked into the bedroom as Mikey called, "It's gonna be Tata warning you."

Unseen by both the brothers, Cris rolled his eyes heavenward. It promised to be a long morning, and he was working the late shift at Cowboys and Angels.

Bennett walked back into the living area with his phone to his ear. He wore the pinched look Cris was starting to hate. "Yes, he's here. What did you say? I know she wouldn't, but you should have warned me…. Yes, I know she's upset. Let me…. Okay, later." He huffed and threw his phone onto the coffee table. "He expects me at three p.m. too."

"What the fuck happened?" Mikey demanded. "What did you say to them?"

"I told them I was gay and Cris was my boyfriend."

Mikey's jaw dropped. "Why the hell did you do that? Are you fucking nuts?"

Bennett took on a mutinous look. "I'm not going to live out the rest of my life as a lie."

"Dammit, you didn't need to tell them. You only needed to say Cris was a friend."

"There's more, Mikey," Cris said quietly from the doorway. "Shut up and listen."

Mikey turned, and something in Cris's face made him pull back. "Go on."

"They know about you too," Bennett said.

"You told them?"

"Not exactly."

"What the fuck exactly?" Mikey's face flushed red, and he clenched his fists.

"They both knew or suspected. Tata was very calm. Mama… she lost it, tried to throw me out. But Hannah said if I went, she'd go too."

Mikey stared at Bennett in horror. "Hannah knows?"

"For fuck's sake," Cris snapped. "The mistake you two make is thinking everyone is stupid." He suddenly remembered Mr. Petrovski's words from the day before.

"Stay out of it," Mikey snarled.

"No." Bennett glared at his brother. "He's right. We spend all our time thinking no one will suspect us. How can they not suspect when you're picking fights and being an ass to Julianne? I'm so busy trying to be the perfect son and pretending I haven't found the woman of my dreams. I've found the *man* of my dreams, and I'm not about to lose him because of our lies. I'm not a celebrity. Yeah, guys like us work with some guys who are homophobes, but guess what? I can hold my own, and they can fuck off and work elsewhere if necessary. They know about Dan and Gideon. Most of them know Cris now. I'm not you. I've never wanted to fall in love with a woman and have a family. What I want is Cris. And if he'll have me, that's what I'm going to do."

"It's not that easy," Mikey growled.

"It *is* that easy. At least this part is. They know I'm gay. Hannah and Adam have my back. Cris is by my side. What about you?"

"You just wait until you can't get guys for the jobs, until they refuse to work for a faggot."

"It's time you got over yourself," Cris snapped. "Those guys you're talking about? They drink at Cowboys and Angels. They're served by me, and Dan, and Gideon. If they had an issue, they'd go drinking elsewhere. Give them fucking credit for being in the twenty-first century."

"If that did happen, I'd leave Petrovski," Bennett said quietly, "but I don't think it will."

Cris studied Bennett's face. He was pale but resolute. Bennett caught his gaze and nodded. He had made his stand, and he wasn't backing down.

"You'd leave?" Mikey looked shocked. "What about Tata?"

"He's always put the business first. He'd find someone to take my place if it were necessary. Maybe Adam or Hannah."

Mikey shook his head vehemently. "They couldn't do half the job you do."

"Thanks, Mikey." Bennett smiled at his brother.

"You leave, and I leave."

Cris snorted. "Is this a family thing?"

At Mikey's confused look, Bennett said, "Hannah said the same thing."

Mikey grunted. "Good."

Cris went to get the coffee and brought it in to hear Bennett say, "You've been wanting to leave for a long time. Maybe now's the time to do it."

"I can't," Mikey said. "You know that."

"Why not?" Cris asked as he handed out the coffee.

"No money."

Cris grunted and took a sip. The heat and caffeine spread through his system and damn, it felt good.

"What about me investing in your company?" Bennett asked.

The naked desire to say yes was clear on Mikey's face before he shook his head. "You can't do that."

"I can, and I will. Mikey, you're a talented craftsman. You've got the potential to be a great one. Do what you want to do. Let me help you."

"What about the business?"

"Petrovski will survive. We have good people working for us."

Cris listened to the exchange with increasing frustration. Yet again, Bennett was putting his brother's needs and desires before his own. Why didn't he ever put himself first? Then he glanced at Bennett's face and realized that was Bennett's raison d'être—the chance to give Mikey what he wanted made him truly happy.

"What will Tata say?"

Bennett wrapped his hands around the hot mug. "We'll find out this afternoon. But Mikey, you've got to face up to the truth."

"You mean Julianne?" Mikey muttered.

"I mean yourself."

"It's so hard. I don't want to hurt her."

"You're hurting her now, dude," Cris said. "And everyone else, including yourself. Mikey, you're gonna end up in jail if you carry on this way. You're not a pretty blonde chick. You're a big man, and you can't bat your eyelashes and expect them to give you a pass."

Mikey grimaced. "Wow, don't hold back."

"I'm not. Bennett's been protecting you for too long. It's time to grow up, Mikey-boy. Face what you are and do the decent thing. Julianne deserves a boyfriend who wants all of her, not just a beard."

"She's not a beard. I love her."

"Not in the right way," Cris said. "You're looking for guys to fuck before you've even set the date."

Bennett gave his brother a wan smile. "Cris is right."

"You would agree with him," Mikey said, his tone petulant.

"Grow up, Mikey," Bennett snapped. "I can't keep pulling you out of the fire. You have to face up to reality. We keep telling you that, but you're not listening."

Mikey drained the last of his coffee and slammed his mug on the table with such force Cris expected it to crack. "What am I gonna tell our parents?"

"That's up to you, but how about the truth?" Cris suggested.

"They already know," Bennett pointed out. "It's not gonna be a surprise. I'll be there this afternoon. I have your back."

Mikey smiled grimly. "I need to see Julianne first."

"Do you want me to come with you?" Bennett asked.

"You need to go to work. Can't have two Petrovskis skipping work. I should do this by myself."

He stood, and Bennett did too. They hugged for a moment, and then Mikey pulled back.

"Gotta go."

Cris refilled their coffees as Bennett saw his brother out of the apartment. When he returned, he looked tired and drawn. He sat next to Cris and murmured his thanks for the refill.

"Is he gonna do it this time?" Cris asked.

"I don't know," Bennett admitted. "He says so."

"Watch this space."

"Indeed." Bennett sighed and finished the drink. "I have to go. I'm already late for a meeting with two of the contractors on the housing project."

"See you later at the bar?"

Bennett kissed Cris on the cheek. "I'll see you there."

Cris turned to give Bennett a proper kiss that left them both breathless. When he pulled back, Bennett took a moment to focus on him and licked his lips.

"Umm."

"You're welcome. Go to work." Cris was pleased to see that all parts of Bennett had enjoyed the kiss.

The apartment seemed empty when he left, and Cris wandered around for a while, wondering what to do. He could go back to bed but that didn't appeal when Bennett wasn't there. He considered going to the gym, but the thought of his peaceful studio won out, and he showered and dressed. He'd spend the day on Bennett's portrait instead of worrying about him.

CRIS ARRIVED at Cowboys and Angels fifteen minutes before his shift. Dan waved at him as he walked past, and Bradley yelled out "About time" as a greeting. He said hi to Dan, flipped Bradley off, and headed into the back.

After he shed his coat, Cris checked his phone again, but he had no missed calls. He'd been waiting for a call from Bennett after his meeting with his father, but there was nothing, not even a text. The rational part of him knew Bennett might still be in the meeting with his dad and Mikey. He imagined there was a lot to talk about. Unfortunately the part of him that spent the day wanting to rush over to be by Bennett's side was the one most vocal. He could call Bennett or text, just check he was okay. But he knew it wasn't his business. The Petrovskis needed to work it out between them. They didn't need Cris interfering.

Still, he could just send a text. Bennett didn't need to reply to it. His phone was in his hands before he had time to consciously process it.

You okay?

Cris stared at the screen, but there was no reply, so he put his phone in his pocket. Later. He'd talk to him later.

He had one foot out the door when his phone beeped, and he stopped to look at the screen.

Yep talk later

As an answer it lacked clarity, but at least Bennett was able to respond. Cris slipped his phone back into his pocket and went to work.

"NEXT!"

Cris's tone was sharper than he intended, but it had been a long evening full of guys determined to try his last nerve. His mom used to say that to him, and now he knew what it meant. His customer service skills had deserted him several hours earlier.

"Hey."

The familiar voice made Cris focus. He looked along the bar and smiled for the first time when Bennett smiled back at him.

"Bad evening?"

"Not now you're here," Cris said. "I am so happy to see you."

"Can you take a break?"

Cris looked over to Dan, who was talking to Gideon. "Hey, can I take my break now?"

Dan spotted Bennett and waved at him. "Hey, Bennett. Sure, it's quiet at the moment."

"Let me get my jacket," Cris said.

Five minutes later he was outside the bar, looking anxiously at Bennett. "How did it go?"

Bennett grimaced. "It was the hardest three hours of my life. Let's walk."

They fell into step beside one another and Cris asked, "Your father? What did he say?"

"Uh, long story short, Mikey is no longer engaged to Julianne and is leaving the company with Tata's blessing. Tata accepts my relationship with you. We have to give Mama time."

Cris processed that. "So that's good, right?"

"Apart from Mama, yes. Tata's going to invest in Mikey's business too, on the understanding Mikey gets his shit together. Then we got the safe-sex lecture."

Cris cringed, and Bennett laughed. "Yeah, it was bad enough the first time around. At least he didn't mention getting anyone pregnant."

"What about you? Are you still working for your dad?"

"I offered to leave. He said no. You have to understand Tata is all about family. The Petrovskis come first but he really wants one of us to take over the business someday."

"Do you want to stay?"

Bennett stopped and smiled. "You know, I think I do."

"Okay, then."

Whatever Cris thought about Bennett's position, he couldn't change the situation. Bennett was all about family too. And the old man had accepted their relationship. He wondered how much Charles's revelation had to do with his acceptance. Cris could work on Mrs. Petrovski. It would take time, but he had patience.

CHAPTER 19

BENNETT SPRAWLED in the mess of the bed like a stranded long-limbed starfish. His eyes were shut, and he snored every so often. Cris rested his head on Bennett's belly, listening to the occasional rumble underneath his ear and content to let him doze. He was tired, but not yet ready to sleep. At some point he'd have to get up and cook, but he was in no rush to move. Every so often Bennett would snort and jump, but then he'd run a warm hand down Cris's back, and the snoring would start again. It was kind of adorable, really. Cris made a mental note to buy earplugs.

He was lost in thought when he realized something was vibrating, so he eased away from Bennett in an effort not to disturb him and rolled off the bed to hunt for his phone. It was buried under a heap of their discarded clothes, and then of course, the vibrating stopped just as he picked it up. When he pressed the button, Cris discovered he'd missed a call from Gideon. He really hoped Gideon didn't need him to take a shift at Cowboys and Angels that evening. The only plan Cris had was to spend it wrapped around his lover, preferably naked.

"Hey." Cris spoke quietly as he left the bedroom, not wanting to wake Bennett, who still hadn't stirred.

"Lionman!" Gideon boomed in his ear, so loudly Cris had to hold the phone away from his head and smack his ear a couple of times to stop it ringing.

"Is everything okay?" he asked as he cautiously put the phone back to his ear.

In the background he could hear Ariel talking to someone and music Cris couldn't initially place. It sounded like something from the eighties. He smiled wryly when the words *lion*, *sleeps*, and *tonight* came together. He should have recognized that straight off. The damn song had haunted him his entire life. His parents had video of him dancing to it when he was a child.

Gideon interrupted his thoughts. "Yeah, it's fine. But I need to talk to you. When's your next shift? Dan's not here, and he's got the staff roster on his laptop."

Cris grinned. "You mean you don't have the password."

"I can see you laughing," Gideon grumbled. "Yeah, he's changed the password."

"You know it's to stop you interfering with the schedule. I'm working tomorrow evening from eight."

"Can you come by the bar before then? I need to talk to you, and it'll be easier if Dan's not hassling me to let you work."

Cris yawned, scratched his belly, and headed to his coffee maker. "Uh, okay. I'll come over in the morning. I've got laundry to do."

"Not today?"

"I'm… busy." The delay was Cris deciding what flavor coffee he wanted, but Gideon gave a bark of laughter.

"Busy? Oh right, say hi to Bennett."

"I will when he wakes up."

"I'm awake," a sleepy voice announced. "Is there coffee?"

Cris looked over his shoulder to see Bennett shuffling toward him, gloriously nude and his eyes half-closed. Cris's dick stirred just at the sight of his sleek, powerful body.

"Gimme a moment," he said to Bennett, and he resisted the urge to fall to his knees and worship at Bennett's cock. "Gideon says hi."

"No, you can't work tonight. You're gonna fuck me."

Bennett slumped into the corner of the sofa and closed his eyes. The man really wasn't awake. His usual filters weren't in place.

Cris smiled and focused his attention on the call. "Bennett says—"

"I heard him." Gideon chuckled again. "Y'all have a great night, and I'll see you in the morning."

"Thanks, Gideon."

He heard Gideon's snicker as they disconnected, but he didn't care. Phone call finished, Cris focused on the task at hand—coffee, not sex—and within a couple of minutes, they sat together on opposite corners of the sofa, legs entwined.

It took Bennett until he'd finished his coffee before he opened one eye to look at Cris. "What did Gideon want?"

"He wants to talk before I go to work tomorrow."

"Oh?"

Cris shook his head. "I don't know why. He didn't say. It's Monday. I do my laundry. I'll go in after that."

"Do you want to go there this evening?" Bennett sounded like it was the last thing he wanted to do.

"You already told Gideon what we're doing this evening." Cris deliberately let need bleed into his voice. He put down his cup and stared intently at Bennett, and it didn't escape his attention that Bennett's dick stirred against his thigh. "What did you say I had to do?"

"I said you have to fuck me," Bennett said hoarsely.

"You'd rather I went to the bar than fuck you?"

"No."

Cris watched Bennett's cock thicken in anticipation. His own body was just as happy at the thought, and he spread his legs to show Bennett.

"Fuck me now," Bennett demanded.

"Put down your cup."

Bennett did as he was told, and Cris crawled over to him and straddled his thighs. The crisp hair tickled Cris's butt.

"You might find it difficult to fuck me like this," Bennett pointed out.

"We have a ways to go before that happens."

"We do?"

Cris kissed him tenderly. "Oh yeah, a long way."

BENNETT HAD a hitch in his gait as he left the next morning. He'd grumbled long and loud, but as Cris watched him walk to the bathroom, he felt unbearably smug. Bennett growled at him, and that made Cris chuckle.

Bennett was almost out the front door when Cris remembered something.

"Wait," he said, and he rushed over to a drawer in the kitchen.

"I'm going to be late for work," Bennett called out.

"I'll be quick, I promise." Cris pushed around the contents until he found what he was looking for. "Aha."

He loped back to Bennett and took his hand. "I want you to take these."

Bennett looked down at the set of keys Cris had dropped into his gloved hand. "Keys to here?"

Cris nodded. "I want you to be able to come and go as you please."

"I... wow, keys. This is a big deal." Bennett closed his fingers around them. "Are you sure?"

"I'm sure."

"I'll get keys cut for my place today." Bennett blinked hard, his eyes suspiciously bright.

Cris kissed him and pushed him out of the door. "Get to work. Can't have two of us fired."

"Call me to let me know what Gideon wants," Bennett said as he walked to the elevator.

He still walked funny and Cris's smugness level increased.

Back in his apartment, Cris stripped the mattress, dumped the sheets in his laundry bag, and remade the bed.

Just after eleven, Cris left the laundromat and headed to Cowboys and Angels. He wrapped up against the weather as a sudden snowstorm had dumped a few inches on the streets. The city hadn't shut down yet, but a lot more snow was forecast. He looked up at the white sky and begged it silently to get lost. If there was significant snow, the bar would shut, and that would mean no money. He couldn't afford to take another financial hit.

Dan waved Cris over as he entered the bar. "Morning. I'll let Gideon know you're here, and then I'll get you a drink."

"Thanks."

Dan used the phone behind the bar to contact Gideon, and then he came back. "What can I get you?"

"Is your coffee machine working?"

The recently installed coffee machine was more temperamental than Gideon's daughter. The staff had started to call the machine Ariel Junior. Not in her or Gideon's earshot, of course.

"Gideon threatened the company if they didn't get Junior sorted. What do you want?"

Cris waited but Dan didn't say any more. He knew Gideon had fingers in many pies, and he supposed Gideon could cause the company a lot of bad exposure if he wanted.

"Hot chocolate would be great."

"Cream and marshmallows?"

Cris would work it off at the gym later. "Sure."

"Lionman! You made it."

One day Gideon would remember his name. One day.

He stood to shake Gideon's hand, and Gideon sat down on the stool next to Cris as Dan placed the chocolate on the bar. This time Cris didn't offer to pay, figuring Gideon had asked him to come in. He took a swallow of the chocolate and wiped away the inevitable creamy mustache.

Gideon took a moment and then said, "I've got a proposition for you."

"Don't tell me, you want a strip night at Cowboys and Angels."

Gideon snorted. "As gorgeous as you are, I think our customers would prefer boobs to dick."

"You're probably right."

"You're on the right lines, though. I've bought Forbidden Nightz."

Cris choked on a marshmallow and took a long time to stop coughing. Tears streamed down his cheeks, and Dan handed him a tissue to mop his eyes and blow his nose.

"Have you finished? Do you know you go almost the color of your hair when you do that?" Gideon had a smug grin on his face.

"You've done what?" Cris managed to gasp out.

"I bought the club. We signed the papers yesterday. And the first thing I did was fire the manager. What a useless piece of crap. How the heck did he get away with running the place like that for so long?"

Cris stared at him, his jaw open. "You fired Marlon? Who's gonna run the place now?"

"You are."

"I… what?"

Gideon frowned. "You seemed more intelligent than this."

"Leave him alone," Dan chided. "Give him a moment to realize you're his boss. It's a big thing."

Gideon smirked at him. "I thought we weren't gonna talk about my big thing, darlin'."

"Guys, please." Cris did not need his new—or same, if he counted the bar—boss discussing the size of his dick at this time in the morning. To give himself time to process Gideon's... it sounded more like an order than a request, he took a drink of his chocolate and managed to get it down without choking.

"Sorry." Gideon couldn't have looked less apologetic if he tried—smug, yes, apologetic, no.

Cris rolled his eyes. "You've fired the manager of the club I no longer work for, and you want to make me the replacement."

"Yes," Gideon said simply.

"I have no experience."

"I do, and so does Dan. You don't have to do this by yourself. I'm not throwing you to the wolves."

Cris had to be grateful for small mercies. "Why me?"

"Because the club needs someone organized at the helm. It can't survive much longer."

"It's in trouble?"

"It was," Gideon corrected. "Now it has a new chance."

"I need training. And the club needs more than a makeover. It needs new guys. We need to hold auditions with new routines. Maybe change what we offer like what Dan's doing here."

Gideon's lips twitched. "You'll take the job?"

Before Cris could answer, Dan interrupted. "Don't commit if you need time to think about it. Gideon forgets people need time to consider their options. He's always fifteen steps ahead of everyone else."

"Darlin', the man's already committed me to renovating the club. He's taking the job." Gideon sounded so sure of himself.

Cris needed to think. It was huge to go from a stripper to the manager. It wasn't that he couldn't do the job, but it would require his careful thought and a long discussion with Bennett. It was a shame his mouth had other ideas. "I'll do it, if you're prepared to put the money in."

"Deal. We're gonna need to close the club for several weeks in January. I've checked the schedule, and it's quiet then."

Cris scowled at Gideon, realizing he was several steps ahead of him already.

"If the club closes, what about the staff? We can't afford to be out of work. Raymond's got another kid on the way."

"I told you that would be the first thing he'd worry about," Dan said.

Gideon nodded, but he focused his attention on Cris. "I'll offer them temporary contracts in other work. They won't earn as much, but at least they'll be employed. There's nothing to stop them going elsewhere if they want to."

"All the staff?"

"All of them."

"What about the bookings?"

"You and I'll deal with those."

There was much more Cris had to think about. He didn't know the first thing about being a manager.

"Hey." Dan snapped his fingers and pulled Cris from his thoughts.

"Huh?"

"You're freaking out."

Cris opened his mouth to deny it and then shut it again. Dan was right. He *was* freaking out.

"Take a deep breath," Dan advised. "It'll all work out. Gideon'll teach you how to run the place."

Gideon squeezed Cris's arm. "I asked you because you can do the job."

Cris inhaled as he was told, exhaled slowly, and looked at Gideon. "Thanks for having faith in me."

"You're welcome."

"Why did you buy the club?"

Gideon nodded at Dan, who'd wandered away to serve a customer. "He told me to. Said it would give me something else to think about, rather than interfering here."

Dan huffed. "That's not what I said."

"You didn't say it with words, darlin', but that's what you meant."

For the dominant one in their relationship, Gideon spent a lot of time doing what Dan wanted him to do. Cris thought it was sweet. He also knew Gideon would kill him if he ever mentioned it.

"Marlon was an asshole. Cris has had more ideas in the last five minutes than Marlon probably had in his entire life." Dan rejoined them. "You bought the club because you know it's got potential. Don't deny it."

Gideon huffed, but finally he nodded. "It will fit in my entertainment and media holdings."

"A strip club," Cris said doubtfully.

"I own casinos and strip clubs elsewhere. Cowboys and Angels is my home, but my media and entertainment companies are diverse."

Dan rolled his eyes and grinned at Cris. "The dude has more fingers in more pies than you'll ever know, but puritanical, he ain't."

"I never thought for a moment that Gideon was puritanical," Cris assured them.

"You'll do fine. Just listen to us, and you'll be okay, Cris," Gideon said.

Cris stared at him, startled. "You know my name?"

"I just like hearing you huff every time I yell out Lionman."

"One day I'm gonna kill you," Cris muttered under his breath, but obviously not low enough, because Gideon smirked.

"I'm your boss, remember?"

"You think that's gonna stop me?"

Dan burst out laughing. "You'll fit in just fine, Cris. And if you have any issues, you can come to me. I know how to handle the big boss." He waggled his eyebrows at Gideon.

"And what happens if I have a problem with you?" Cris asked.

"You don't," Gideon said flatly. "No one has a problem with Dan and lives to tell the tale." He exchanged a heated look with Dan.

"What the hell am I doing?" Cris asked to the room at large.

Dan pushed over a shot glass and filled it with bourbon. "Drink up, man. You'll need this. You've got a long day ahead of you. Gideon's taking you to the club for a few hours before your shift here tonight."

"My laundry—"

"You've got five minutes," Gideon growled, "and that includes making a phone call to your boyfriend. Then we'll collect your laundry."

Cris was pulling out his phone even as Gideon spoke. "On it, boss."

"As I said, you'll do just fine," Gideon purred.

CHAPTER 20

CRIS WENT into a corner of Cowboys and Angels and called Bennett. After three rings Bennett answered and Cris broke the news to him.

"That's great," Bennett enthused.

Cris blinked. Bennett sounded very laid-back. Maybe he hadn't heard him. That could have been due to the volume of noise at Bennett's end from shouting and large machinery, but Cris had to check.

"Did you hear what I said?" Cris asked.

"Yes. Gideon's bought Forbidden Nightz and made you the manager."

"And you don't mind?"

"Why should I mind?" Bennett sounded genuinely confused.

"Bennett, this is a big deal. He's made me manager—"

"Wait a minute." Suddenly the noise was muted, and Bennett sighed in relief. "Sorry, I was halfway across the site when you called. Now, where were we?"

"Club. Manager—"

"Oh yeah. You're freaking out."

"I am not freaking out," Cris objected.

"Uh-huh." Bennett couldn't have projected a more disbelieving tone if he tried.

"Okay, I'm freaking out. But this is huge, and I'm going to be working all hours. This affects us."

"Yeah, I know. But it's not like I can't join you at the club when you're working, and part of being a good manager is to delegate. You'll need an assistant manager. What about Raymond?"

"You think so?" Cris hadn't thought about that.

"We're getting ahead of ourselves here, but I'm used to running a team. I can help. I'm sure Gideon is going to stick his nose in, and you've got several weeks before it opens."

Cris took a deep breath. Bennett was right. No point running before he could walk. They would sort out the hours, and it wasn't as though Bennett didn't work… wait. "You already knew about this, didn't you?"

"I—"

"Don't you dare lie to me, Bennett Petrovski. How did you know?"

"It's not some great big conspiracy, Cris. Gideon talked to Tata, who told Mikey, who told me. Only yesterday. I didn't know he was going to offer you the job."

"But you didn't tell me."

"I was distracted. You distracted me. Your dick distracted me."

Cris huffed loudly at Bennett's feeble protest. "My dick ain't that powerful. Gideon buys my former club and fires the manager, and you don't tell me?"

"Well—"

"Yes?" Cris snapped.

"Okay, I thought there might be a chance Gideon would offer you your old job, and I wanted it to be a surprise. I never thought he'd offer you the manager's job."

"He's agreed to refurbish the club—new stage, new structures, everything."

"His idea?"

"Uh… I suggested it. Along with new guys and new routines."

"You see? He made the right choice."

"Are you sure?"

Cris was suddenly insecure, and he needed Bennett's reassurance—he needed his *boyfriend's* reassurance.

"I'm more than sure," Bennett said soothingly. "Where are you now?"

"At the bar. I've got to go. Gideon's anxious to get to the club."

Gideon had been sitting by the bar, jacket across his lap, waiting patiently for Cris to finish his call. Now his jacket was on, and he stared at Cris.

"I'll talk to you later. Tell me how it goes."

"I will." Cris mumbled a "love you."

"I love you too."

Cris would never get over hearing that from Bennett. He slipped his phone in his pocket and joined Gideon at the bar. "I'm ready."

"Bennett okay about it?" Gideon asked.

Cris nodded. "Turns out he knew about the sale of the club. I wonder how he knew that?" He turned his best wide-eyed innocent stare on Gideon, who just shrugged.

"You want something to get around you tell one of the Petrovskis. I thought he'd tell you."

"Not a word."

"I'll remember that in future. Let's go."

"Be back by five," Dan called from the other end of the bar, where he had been frowning at his laptop for the last fifteen minutes.

"He works for me now," Gideon pointed out in a far too mild tone.

"Tough," Dan snapped. "I need him until I get a replacement."

Cris sighed. "I can work for both of you, at least for a while." His art would have to wait.

"Boy, if you work for me, you're not gonna have time to scratch your pert butt," Gideon boomed.

Dan fixed his husband with a hard stare. "You think Cris has a pert butt?"

Gideon looked like a deer trapped in headlights.

"It's time to go," Cris said and hustled Gideon out of the door. Cris looked over to see Dan smirking at them, so he smirked back. It was good to see Gideon shut up. Cris had a feeling that didn't happen nearly enough.

FORBIDDEN NIGHTZ was empty. Gideon had the key to the entrance in the alley, and he held the door open to let Cris through.

"I've gotten keys for you in the office."

"I can't believe you fired Marlon," Cris murmured as they walked through to the tiny office and their footsteps echoed in the silence of the club. That was odd in itself. Marlon had always had the radio on during the daytime. The place smelled different too, its usual heavy scent of women's perfumes and male sweat a distant memory. Cris shook himself. The club had been closed for one day, for heaven's sake.

Gideon grunted. "He was useless. I was going to give him a chance, but he had no ideas for the club. He was more interested in how to bed the strippers than how to improve business."

Cris had been on the receiving end of Marlon's charms when he first started at the club, but it hadn't taken him too long to realize the manager just wanted to fuck him. Cris said no. That's why Marlon always fucked with his schedule and no one else's, but Cris could never prove it.

"He offered me the choice of whoever I wanted." Gideon grimaced, obviously disgusted. "He even offered your ass for sale."

"And what did you say to that?"

"That if he said one more word I'd make him sorry." His face and voice were grim, and Cris knew he meant every word.

"I turned him down," Cris said.

Gideon rolled his eyes. "I think that was obvious. Let's get started. Dan'll kill me if I get you back late."

Cris nodded and pointed to the stage. "Let's start over there, and I'll tell you my plans."

"This is going to bankrupt me, isn't it?"

"I hope so," Cris said cheerfully as he took Gideon to the main stage.

He had plans—big plans—and unlike Marlon, he knew exactly how to make them happen. When they dropped his bag of clean clothes at his apartment, Cris had picked up his camera and a lined pad and pencils so he could approach the remodel like one of his paintings. He flipped open the pad and picked up a pencil.

"Gideon, you make the coffee, and I'll show you what I have in mind for the stage," he ordered. He didn't register the fact that he was ordering his new boss around until Gideon had vanished into the staff kitchen area.

By the time Gideon returned with two steaming mugs of coffee, Cris had sketched out the main stage, the new structures, and where the audience would sit.

Gideon handed him a mug and studied the drawings. "Have you seen this before?"

"Yep, and it works really well. The audience likes it too."

"I've got something similar in another club of mine. The plans are in my office."

"Good. Then we won't be starting from scratch. What do you think of the backstage area? This one's only rough." He handed Gideon another plan.

"I think I picked the right person for the job."

Cris looked up and smiled at Gideon. "Thank you for giving me the chance."

He took photo after photo of the club from every angle and he sent Gideon out to get a tape measure too, ignoring Gideon's pointed "Today was to get ideas, not finalize details."

Gideon shut up when Cris growled that this was how he worked, and if Gideon didn't like it, he could find someone else to do the job. Finally, when he had all the information he needed, he took pity on Gideon and they drove back to Cowboys and Angels.

As they parked outside the club, Cris turned to Gideon. "When do we start?"

Gideon looked confused. "I thought we already had."

Cris shook his head. "No, I mean when do I start as manager?"

"You already have."

"Then we need to discuss salary, and I can't keep working at the bar. This is gonna take me time to design."

"I have people who do that," Gideon pointed out, although Cris could see a smile playing around his lips.

"I do it, or you find someone else to be manager."

"How did I end up with two of you?" Gideon complained.

"Huh?" Cris stared at him, confused.

"You and Dan. You're both the same."

"You're a very lucky man, Gideon. Now, are you gonna tell Dan you've just swiped his new bartender or am I?"

"Do tonight's shift, and I'll tell him."

"Done." Cris had planned to do that anyway. He wouldn't leave Dan in the lurch.

"He's not going to be happy," Gideon grumbled as he slid out of the car.

Cris winced as the first icy snowflakes stung his cheeks. "Tell him it's his fault. It was his suggestion."

Gideon brightened. "I can't wait to see his face when I tell him that."

"Just make sure I'm somewhere else."

"Coward."

"I like my skin intact."

"Speaking of... do you think you'll want to carry on as Lionman?"

Cris thought about for a moment. "Maybe to teach the new guys, or if we're desperate for an act. But I think maybe Marlon was right—it's time to let the new guys in."

"You're only twenty-five," Gideon pointed out. "Raymond is older than you."

"I know, and I love Lionman. But you're giving me the chance to do something new. As long as Bennett deals with the hours and I can still paint, I'll be happy." He scuffed a star into the falling snow on the sidewalk. "The money's not such an issue now."

"Are you moving in with Bennett?"

Cris rolled his eyes. "You're giving me a salary, remember?"

"Oh yeah. We'd better go talk about that."

Cris followed Gideon into the bar. Gideon was about to discover his new manager was no slouch in the negotiating department either.

BENNETT WAS asleep in his bed when Cris arrived home. That was a welcome surprise. Bennett had a key but the fact that he was there, in his bed, even though Cris was working late, made their relationship seem more real.

Bennett was also in the middle of the bed again. Cris contemplated sleeping on the sofa, but he was tired and cold, and he wanted to sleep around his boyfriend. So he stripped down to his briefs, edged under the covers, and gently nudged Bennett over to one side. Bennett grumbled, but he moved and let Cris wrap around him.

"You're freezing," he complained.

"You should feel my feet."

Cris slid them down Bennett's legs, and Bennett yelped, but he didn't shove Cris away.

"I hate you."

"No, you don't." Cris kissed the warm, slightly sweaty nape of Bennett's neck.

"No, I don't," Bennett mumbled, and he was asleep on the next snore.

Cris smiled, pressed his cold cheek against Bennett's shoulder, and let the warmth lull him into a deep sleep.

The next time he woke, Cris was alone in the bed, apart from a pale pink rose on the next pillow. He picked up the rose and sniffed it. Then he sat up and saw the note the rose had been resting on. The writing was hard to read.

"You write like a spider hurled over the page," Cris muttered, but his smile was tender.

I didn't want to wake you.

I'll call you later.

I love you. The rose is to keep you company until I return.

You snore!

"You old romantic, you."

Cris held the rose as he scurried out of his bedroom and into the kitchen. Bennett had obviously cranked up the space heater because the apartment was warmer than he usually kept it. As he was only dressed in briefs, Cris appreciated Bennett's thoughtfulness. He placed the rose in a large glass and filled it with water. Cris had never received flowers before, and he didn't have a suitable vase.

Then he looked at the time. Ten thirty. He wasn't due in until the evening. After a heated discussion with Dan, he and Gideon agreed Cris would finish his week at Cowboys and Angels, and after that, he was free to take up his new role as manager of Forbidden Nightz. Cris was going to change the name of the club. He didn't know to what yet, but it was going to happen.

Cris stroked one of the pale pink petals. "You constantly surprise me, Bennett Petrovski. I never took you for a romantic."

He had a lot to learn about his boyfriend, and he looked forward to finding out every last detail.

BENNETT GROANED and threw his head back. Only Cris's quick reflexes saved him from being hit in the face. He'd pinned Bennett, face against the wall and wrists above his head as soon as he walked through the door.

"Sorry," Bennett gasped out.

"Tell me what you want." Cris's breath caressed the shell of Bennett's ear.

Bennett pushed back against Cris's groin. "Fuck me."

"Where?"

"Here. Now."

"Keep your hands where they are," Cris ordered.

Bennett moaned again, but he obeyed and stayed in position as Cris reached around to undo the button of Bennett's jeans and push them and his briefs down to his knees. Cris's mouth went dry as Bennett's taut, fuzzy butt was exposed. He pushed up Bennett's shirt, ran his hand down his spine, and cupped one asscheek.

"You feel so good," Cris moaned. Bennett tried to thrust back, but Cris kept him in place with one hand between his shoulder blades. "I'm doing the driving."

"You're going to drive me insane," Bennett muttered.

"Good."

Cris fumbled in his pants pocket for a condom and lube, and Bennett gave a bark of laughter when he heard the *snick* of the cap on the lube.

"I do like a man who's prepared."

"I'm always prepared."

Tight heat gripped his fingers as Cris pushed into Bennett's hole, and Bennett groaned loudly. Cris had quickly learned that Bennett was a noisy lover, which was fine because just listening to him moan made Cris hard. He wished he was prepared enough to push his jeans down first, because his dick was trying to drill a hole through his zipper.

It didn't take long to make Bennett good and ready for him. He keened as Cris withdrew his fingers, wiped them on his jeans, and made soothing noises as he shoved his jeans down and gloved his shaft as quickly as he could with shaking fingers.

"Hurry up," Bennett ordered. "You have to hurry up."

"Almost there, baby, almost there."

He hoped Bennett was so far gone that he'd missed the endearment, but Bennett growled in the back of his throat. "Not your baby."

Cris lined up behind Bennett, palmed his ass because he loved the feel of the flexing muscle under his hands, and pushed in. He was gloriously familiar with Bennett's body now, and he knew when to push and when to hold, when to wait for sweat to break between Bennett's shoulder blades and trickle down his back ready for Cris to lick the trail back up his spine.

They were both panting hard by the time Cris was ready to move. He wanted to reach around to feel the hardness of Bennett's shaft, feel it leak over his fingers, but his control was slipping.

"You're gonna have to jack off, because I'm so close," he said.

"Don't need to," Bennett bit out.

The jeans still hampered them, and the angle wasn't quite right, but Cris tugged on Bennett's hips. Then Bennett stuck his ass out more, and Cris thrust home with a shout of relief. The next couple of minutes was a blur of pushing and grunting, slapping of body on body. Cris's head filled with the sheer need to climax, his orgasm coiling and ready to strike. He wanted to wait for Bennett to come first, but his body won out, and he slammed into Bennett's welcoming greedy ass with a shout of relief. He pumped come into the condom and wished there was nothing between them.

In the one part of his mind that was still aware, he felt Bennett come, and the tight muscle clenched around his body and drew his orgasm out. Then Bennett's legs gave way, and Cris tried keeping their balance, but they collapsed to the ground in a hot, sticky mess of wobbly legs and jeans. In a valiant effort, Cris managed not to land on Bennett, which was a miracle.

Bennett turned to sit up against the wall, wearily kicked off his sneakers, and shucked his jeans and briefs. Cris attempted to do the same, although he was still come-drunk and everything took twice as long. Bennett slapped his hands away, stripped him of his pants and briefs, and staggered into the bathroom with the condom.

Cris stayed where he was, eyes closed, until Bennett joined him again and slid down to lay his head on Cris's lap. He carded his fingers through Bennett's hair and contemplated what a lucky man he was.

He had a boyfriend and a new job—a scary, amazing, challenging job.

"I'm so damn lucky," he said quietly, not wanting to disturb the satiated peace.

"We both are." Bennett pressed a kiss into Cris's thigh.

"There is one thing I wish."

Bennett didn't move. He just murmured, "Oh?"

Cris fidgeted. "I wish I hadn't sat in the wet patch."

He felt rather than heard Bennett's snicker.

EPILOGUE

THE FIRST beats of his intro music sounded, the spotlights crossed the redesigned stage, the noise from the audience dipped for a fraction, and the Lionman strutted to the front. He stared out, and the look in his eyes and the jut of his hips challenged the audience he could barely see under the stage lights. His blood pulsed as he tipped his cowboy hat, and the women in the audience roared. Oh yeah. This was what he was here for. He pumped his fist, and they went wild.

The Lionman was the opening act for the sold-out first night of Mane Events. True to Gideon's word, the club had been gutted and redesigned with Cris's input. It had taken much longer than Cris anticipated, but they were back, bolder and in your face. The old stage had been removed and replaced with a round stage with state-of-the-art lighting and moveable structures.

With Mikey Petrovski's help, he'd designed the new stage from top to bottom and pointed out to his father that his engineering degree had finally come in handy. He wasn't entirely joking. Other clubs had approached him to see if he would do the same for them. He was still thinking over their offers. The refurbishment had come at a price and Gideon swore Cris was going to bankrupt him, but Cris ignored his grumbles. Mane Events was going to do more than survive. It was going to be *the* place to go.

"Lionman! Lionman! Lionman!"

They yelled and hollered and chanted his name like a mantra, and the force of his smile increased with every repeat of his name. For the next ten minutes, he was gonna drive those women crazy and tease them the only way the Lionman could.

For the last time.

He slowly stripped off his jacket and teased them with a broad shoulder and a flash of his oiled pecs. Every movement was a challenge. He loved it, and they roared their appreciation.

The music changed, and he started to sway, showing them his pert ass framed by his tight pants. The women shrieked. He turned his head, winked at them, and strutted to the framework to gyrate around it.

He slowly untied his bandana and used it to wipe his face, making love to that small piece of cloth until he tucked it into his back pocket and wriggled his ass again.

Lionman was down to his jeans and cowboy boots as he stalked around the stage to glare at them challengingly. "Is there a birthday girl out there?" A cheer went up in one corner of the room, and he grinned. "Is there a Loopy-Lou here?"

"She's here. She's here," several women screamed at once.

"Oh my God, no, what did you do?" Loopy-Lou, he presumed. Her voice rose above the din.

He left the stage and stalked over to one table as though he were hunting his prey. The crowd seemed to move apart, leaving Loopy-Lou in the center to be caught by the Lionman. She was a beautiful curvaceous woman dressed in a skintight red satin dress.

She looked petrified.

He stood before her and swayed and gyrated until he was on her lap, and she was frozen rigid. Her friends yelled their approval.

Lionman leaned forward to whisper in her ear. "I won't do anything you don't want me to do. Just tap my thigh if you want it to stop. Okay?" Loopy-Lou relaxed a fraction. "I'm gonna take your friend back to my lair," he roared, and he led her to the stage.

He knew just how to work the crowd so they didn't see how gentle he was being with Loopy-Lou, and it was a relief to work with someone who didn't want to grope his balls. He writhed around her, and she ripped off his pants to reveal a shiny red jockstrap. That left him in his jockstrap, hat, jacket, and boots.

As he hid her face, supposedly in his groin, she tucked a Benjamin into his jockstrap. He writhed again and drew her to her feet.

"Okay?" he asked, his smile just for her.

She nodded and managed a smile, her large eyes less petrified than before. "Thank you. I was dreading this."

"I look after my women." He winked and roared, and the crowd roared with him.

Lionman gallantly helped the woman down from the stage and blew her a kiss. She giggled and went back to her seat to be swarmed by her envious friends, and he danced away. Lionman had a routine to finish.

The last note sounded and Lionman, bare-assed naked aside from the jockstrap, strutted off the stage leaving behind the yells and cheers and demands for more. Always leave them wanting.

"They all want a piece of you." Bennett's smile was wry, his words barely audible over the noise of the crowd.

"They want a piece of Lionman." Cris smirked at his boyfriend who'd been watching from the wings. "They ain't getting him, though. He's taken."

Bennett raised an eyebrow. "He is?"

"Uh-uh," Cris said huskily. "He's definitely taken." He tugged Bennett over for a kiss, but his boyfriend wrinkled his nose.

"You need a shower."

"I'm disgusting," Cris agreed, wrinkling his own nose. He was covered in oil and sweat. He pointed to his cheek and Bennett dropped a light kiss before pointing to the shower. He always waited for Cris to shower away "work" before they cuddled.

"You were amazing," Bennett said.

"You're just biased," Cris teased.

"Yeah. Totally biased. But you were."

Cris knew he'd been amazing, but he made a token protest anyway.

Olly grinned as he pushed past them for his set. Cris had kept him on and trained him intensively while the club had been closed. "Leave the man alone, Cris. He's in love."

Cris raised an eyebrow. "Is this true? Who're you in love with?"

"Ass," Bennett said, and popped Cris lightly on the butt. "Go get showered. The others are waiting to celebrate."

"They're here already?"

"Oh yeah. They wanted to see your show. Why're you blushing, Lionman?"

Cris's flush had spread up his chest. "Not Mama and Tata. Please don't tell me your parents watched me strip?"

Bennett snickered. "Tata did ask, but I said no. They're joining us at Cowboys and Angels."

Cris slumped back against the wall. "Thank God for small mercies."

"My sister knows exactly what a lucky man I am, though."

"Did you have to invite them?" Cris whined.

"Cris, it's not every day we get to celebrate you being made manager. Of course, I was going to invite Hannah and Adam."

Cris stared at him in horror. "Adam's here as well?"

"I'll let you into a little secret. Hannah already knew who you were. She's been here before. And she has plenty of pictures, which Adam has seen."

"I'm never gonna live this down," Cris moaned.

"There's nothing to live down. We're all proud of you, Lionman."

"Even though I'm—was—a stripper?" This had been worrying Cris for some time. Mikey was dating a hot detective, but Mr. Petrovski must feel his eldest son could do better than a stripper.

"You're the manager of a brand-new and shit-hot club, and you got that by being a very successful stripper. I'm not ashamed of what you do. It's thanks to you, Mikey and I are finally free to live our lives. You have a golden heart, Lionman."

Bennett looked so serious, Cris had to believe him. Still, there was one last thing he had to know. "I want to concentrate on running the club. Would you be happy with plain old Cris Peters, rather than Lionman?"

"Lionman is for them. He was never mine." Bennett jabbed a thumb in the vague direction of the stage. "I like him, but I love you, and there's nothing plain about you, Cris Peters. Nothing plain at all."

Cris gave him a relieved smile and took his hand. "Let me go shower, then we can go and celebrate."

In the small changing room, Cris dumped the bills that had been in his jockstrap into his lockbox, not bothering to check the amount. He locked it and shoved it in his bag. Then he stripped off his jockstrap and headed to the shower. He'd installed powerful showers, and it was a relief to feel the water washing away the oil and sweat from his body. One of the things he was really looking forward to was never having to subject his body hair to Hans the Torturer again. Cris dumped some shampoo in his hand and soaped his hair, taking his time to come down from the excitement of the set.

Once he was out of the shower, Cris dried off, wrapped a towel around his waist and went back into the changing room. It wasn't that he needed the towel in front of Bennett, but he had been caught out by strangers wandering in before. Sometimes, enterprising women had found their way backstage and Cris was put in the position of explaining that Lionman stripped for the ladies, but Cris Peters preferred guys. Most of the intruders took it well, but one or two had taken his rejection to heart and he'd had to call security.

To his relief, Bennett was on his own waiting for him. Cris dropped the towel, aware of Bennett's heated gaze on his skin. He quickly pulled on his briefs and dress slacks before his body gave him away and they got distracted with other things.

"The others have moved on to Cowboys and Angels," Bennett said as Cris finished dressing. "The parents were threatening to come down, so we decided to meet them there."

"I can't imagine your mama in the bar. It's almost as bizarre as imagining her in here."

"The mistake you're making is thinking my mama is an uptown girl. She's strictly blue-collar stock. She used to work in Cowboys and Angels when they first arrived in New York. That was before Gideon's time."

Cris tried and failed to imagine Mrs. Petrovski behind the bar. "Your parents manage to surprise me every day."

"And that's just the way they like it. Don't ever let them know this, or they'll go all out to impress you. It's not pretty." Bennett shuddered. "Just ask Mikey about the time my father dyed his hair to hide the gray, and then went out in the rain."

"The dye ran?"

"He was applying for a loan at his bank. He had to sit there with his collar brown from the hair dye and convince them he was a professional."

Cris's lips twitched. "Did he get the loan?"

"Yeah he did." Bennett laughed. "And better terms than they were originally going to offer. He ended up talking to the manager about hair dye, and for some reason, she really liked him."

"I can understand that. I've met his eldest son and he's pretty lovable too."

Bennett tugged him in for a kiss, leaving them both breathless. "You know just what to say to make me feel like a million dollars."

Cris ran his thumb over Bennett's lips. "Right back atcha."

Bennett kissed Cris's thumb. "Let's go play nice with the parents because afterwards, I'm going to demand some lion-time."

"I'm never going to be able to forget Lionman, am I?"

"Not with what's in your closet." Bennett twinkled at him. "But he's retired now. No one gets to see what's you're offering. I want private showings."

"I'm all yours, Bennett."

"You can call me Benny if you want."

Cris thought back to their first meeting and the curt insistence that Benny was only for the family. "I don't think of you as Benny. What about Baby?"

Bennett scowled at him. "Never in a million years."

"But you are my baby." Cris smirked at him because he knew Bennett really hated endearments like baby and sweetie.

"I'll end you," Bennett said flatly.

Cris gave a large theatrical sigh. "Oh well, if you insist."

"I do."

Bennett popped Cris on the butt and told him to move. Cris saluted him and then they were heading out of the club. Bennett had ordered a car and it was waiting outside.

Once they were on their way, Cris laid his head on Bennett's shoulder, feeling suddenly exhausted after the adrenaline rush of the set.

"You can't sleep yet," Bennett murmured.

"I'm not sleeping." Cris closed his eyes. "Just dozing. Adrenaline crash."

Bennett stroked Cris's face. "Fine, then. You sleep. I'll wake you when we get there."

Cris hummed and did as he was told.

At Cowboys and Angels, the party looked like it was in full swing. Dan had drafted Gideon into working behind the bar, along with Ariel and her friends. Cris hadn't quite woken up, and he let Bennett push him through the crowd. When Dan waved at him, he waved back, but he was dead on his feet. He hoped the beer didn't knock him flat.

Mr. Petrovski spotted them first and rushed over to shake Cris's hand. "Congratulations on your retirement and your promotion, son. Today is the start of something big for you."

"Thank you, sir." Cris smiled at him. "It went really well."

"So it should," Bennett said. "You prepared for it for long enough."

Cris nodded. He'd left nothing to chance. Still, it was good to hear Bennett say that.

"It won't prevent you from being ready for the July opening, will it?" Mr. Petrovski asked.

Cris stared at him, confused. "The July opening?"

Bennett laughed and slung an arm around Cris's shoulders. "He doesn't know about that, Tata. I thought I'd leave that to you."

"Know about what?" Cris glanced between them.

Mr. Petrovski grunted at his son and then turned to Cris. "Our new building opens in July. You're providing the art."

Cris's eyes opened wide. "Me?" he squeaked. Any vestige of sleep vanished in an instant. He was wide-awake.

"Yes, you." Bennett looked like a small kid finally allowed to reveal a secret. "I showed Tata your construction series, and he thought they'd look great in the lobby of the new building. The building opens with your exhibition."

"That's amazing, but shouldn't you get someone famous? Not a stripper with a paintbrush?" The minute the words hit the air, Cris groaned inwardly. He needed to duct tape his mouth or he was going to talk himself out of the biggest opportunity of his life.

Mr. Petrovski frowned at him and shook his head. "You're going to be my son-in-law. That's good enough for me."

"I am?"

Bennett scowled at his father. "Tata, you're getting ahead of yourself. You know we haven't discussed the *M* word yet." He turned to Cris. "My parents invest a lot of money in upcoming artists. They do this for every new building they open. The Petrovski family is well known for their patronage of the arts."

Cris eyed him a little sourly. "You didn't think to tell me this sooner?"

"I thought it might freak you out."

He had a point. Cris *was* totally freaked out. Then he thought of something. "How did your father see my paintings?"

Bennett had the grace to look embarrassed. "I asked Antonio at your studio if I could bring Tata to look. Turns out they met at an exhibition already."

"I'm going to kill him," Cris muttered. "And then I'll bring him back to hug him."

Mr. Petrovski clapped him on the shoulder. "You come talk to me after tonight. I'll tell you what I want to see in my building. Now let my wife talk to you before she explodes."

He wandered away, and Cris turned to Bennett. "Your mom wants to talk to me now?"

Bennett took his hand and entwined their fingers. "It's okay. You'll be fine. Just take a deep breath."

Cris glowered at him, but he obediently practiced his deep-breathing exercises until she appeared.

"I'll protect you," Bennett whispered.

Mrs. Petrovski looked as immaculate as ever in a cream suit and heels that defied gravity. She hugged Bennett and then turned to Cris. "Congratulations on your new job."

"Thank you, ma'am." He'd never called her Mama after their first meeting.

She gave him a long, steady look. "I know how badly I behaved the first time we met."

Cris kept quiet, because he didn't want to be rude to the woman who might end up his mother-in-law, but he wouldn't forget that encounter. She nodded as though she understood the reason for his silence.

"I love my sons, Cris. But I'll admit it has been hard for me to accept, well, who they are."

"Mama—" Bennett began, but she held up her hand and he trailed off.

"It's okay, Benny. I know this is my problem, not yours. I'll work through it. I don't want to lose my family, and you've all made it clear that will happen. It's hard for me to accept you put someone else first, but even so, you've all made me proud for what strong children I've raised."

I don't like it, but.... Cris would accept that—for now. He held out his hand to Mrs. Petrovski, and she put her hand in his.

"You have a fine family, ma'am."

"Maybe one day you could call me Mama?"

"One day," he agreed.

She left them after another hug with Bennett, and Cris collapsed against him.

"You know I'm going to kill you too, don't you? Your mom and an exhibition? I haven't got time to prepare for this."

Bennett dimpled at him. "You're welcome, and you have more than enough paintings completed for the space. You just need to choose the right ones. Uh… Tata's already picked them out, to be honest."

"Let me guess, they're all Petrovski buildings."

"You got it."

"And what about the one of you?"

Bennett shook his head. "That one's going to a private collection."

"It's on the wall in our bedroom," Cris pointed out.

"And that's where it's going to stay."

Cris shook his head. He wasn't going to argue. Being able to share a bedroom with the man he loved was more than enough. An exhibition, a management job, and a boyfriend? "Pinch me," he said suddenly. Then he yelped when Bennett pinched his ass. "Okay, I'm not dreaming."

"Put him down, Benny," Mikey said. "You can grope him later." He'd appeared out of nowhere, and Ramon's arm was wrapped around his shoulders. They both carried two bottles of beer and handed one each to Bennett and Cris. "Dan sent them over."

Cris turned to the bar and mouthed "thanks" at Dan, who saluted him.

"Well done, Lionman," Ramon said as he tipped his bottle at Cris.

"Former Lionman," Cris corrected. "Now just Cris Peters."

"Congrats on the exhibition," Mikey said, and he raised his own bottle. "You must be good. Tata's very fussy about who he exhibits in his buildings."

Cris turned to Bennett, who nodded.

"He wouldn't have agreed if he hadn't seen your work. He personally picks out each piece of art to go in his buildings."

There was a lump in Cris's throat, and he had to swallow hard to speak. "I don't know what to say."

"Drink your beer," Mikey suggested.

Bennett tipped his bottle at Cris, and his expression promised so much more later. "To my boyfriend, manager and artist. To us."

Cris clinked his bottle with Bennett's. "To us," he said softly. "To us."

SUE BROWN is owned by her dog and two children. When she isn't following their orders, she can be found with her laptop in Starbucks, drinking latte and eating chocolate.

Sue discovered M/M romance at the time she woke up to find two men kissing on her favorite television series. The kissing was hot and tender and Sue wanted to write about these men. She may be late to the party, but she's made up for it since, writing fan fiction until she was brave enough to venture out into the world of original fiction.

Sue can be found at:

Website: www.suebrownstories.com
Blog: suebrownsstories.blogspot.co.uk
Twitter: @suebrownstories
Facebook: www.facebook.com/suebrownstories

SUE BROWN

SPEED DATING the BOSS

COWBOYS & ANGELS

Cowboys and Angels: Book One

Will a mix of privilege and blue collar be a recipe for love… or disaster?

Dan's pretty satisfied with his job at the working-class bar Cowboys and Angels. He enjoys his simple life, his apartment, and his cat, but he could do without the fights that break out in the bar, his boss's meddling daughter, Ariel… oh, and a brutal, unrequited crush on his straight alpha boss, Gideon.

When Dan's friend prepares to tie the knot, everyone insists that Dan needs a date for the wedding. Before he can protest, Ariel arranges a gay speed-dating event at the bar with Gideon as a participant. The unforeseen revelation that Gideon is bisexual raises Dan's hopes, especially when Gideon announces that he wants to accompany Dan to the wedding. Could Gideon really be interested in Dan?

When Dan needs someone most, Gideon offers his unconditional support, and with genuine commitment, he shows Dan the kind of man he really is. Teaming up to save the wedding from a hungover groom and intolerant parents, can Gideon convince Dan they're the best match since beer and pizza?

www.dreamspinnerpress.com

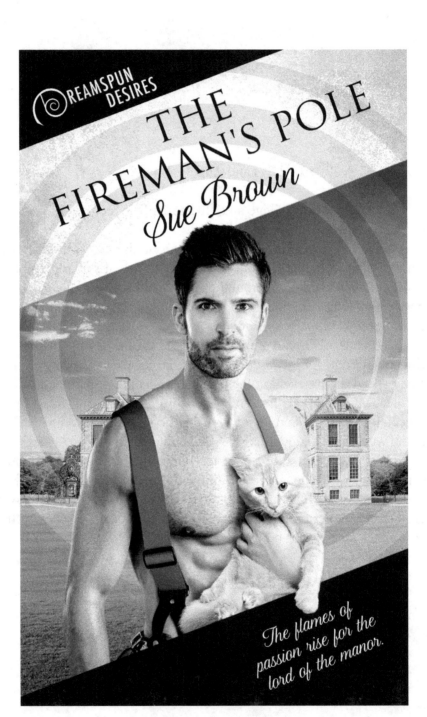

DREAMSPUN
DESIRES

THE
FIREMAN'S POLE
Sue Brown

The flames of
passion rise for the
lord of the manor.

The flames of passion rise for the lord of the manor.

It's springtime in Calminster village, but things are already heating up. Sexy firefighter Dale Maloney is new to the local station. When Dale backs the company fire engine into the village maypole, he attracts the ire—and attention—of Benedict Raleigh, the Baron Calminster.

Soon after meeting Dale, Ben breaks off his relationship with his girlfriend, and the sparks between Ben and Dale are quickly fanned into flames.

Unfortunately the passion between the two men isn't the only blaze in the village. An arsonist's crimes are escalating, and it's up to Dale and his crew to stop them. Meanwhile, as they investigate, an unscrupulous business partner attempts to coerce Ben into marrying his daughter. The May Day parade is around the corner, but they have plenty of fires to put out before Ben can finally slide down the fireman's pole.

www.dreamspinnerpress.com

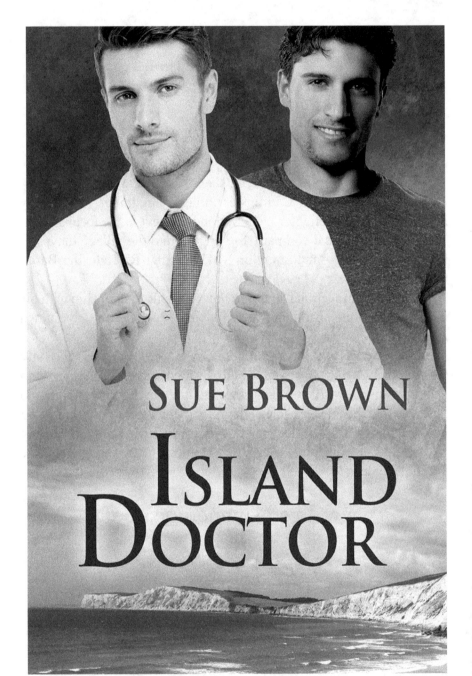

SUE BROWN

ISLAND DOCTOR

Island Medics: Book One
An Isle Novel

Dr. Jeff Martin has spent five years as a rural general practitioner on the Isle of Wight, hiding the fact he's gay. He travels in secret to see his partner, Tris, but when he discovers Tris has been cheating on him, he ends their relationship. Then Jeff meets island native Cameron Gillard. Cameron is down-to-earth, lively, and treats Jeff like he's the most important person in his life. Jeff blooms under Cameron's attention, and he decides to come out to his colleagues and friends.

Just when things are going well, Tris reappears out of the blue. Jeff is no longer interested in Tris, but it seems he has two men to convince. Tris, who can't believe Jeff is serious about wanting to end their relationship, and Cameron, who can't hide his jealousy of Tris.

Jeff is certain about one thing—the only man he wants in his life is Cameron. Now he just needs to prove it to him.

www.dreamspinnerpress.com

The
Next
Call

SUE BROWN

Mark Grayson volunteers for an LGBT helpline, the same one that helped him through his teenage years. One day he takes a call from "Ricky," a suicidal man being forced into a marriage he doesn't want. For weeks Mark talks to Ricky and provides support, but he's frustrated by the lack of information Ricky provides and the decisions he's making. In the meantime, Mark starts a relationship with another volunteer. Then tragedy strikes and Mark takes time away from the helpline, but when he comes back, Ricky is waiting. Mark realizes Ricky is stronger than before and their relationship changes, but Mark isn't sure what their future holds if their relationship is destined to be at the end of the phone.

www.dreamspinnerpress.com

CPSIA information can be obtained
at www.ICGtesting.com
Printed in the USA
LVHW080511101220
673815LV00025B/414

9 781640 806528